SHIFTERS

Catherine Lambourne

ISBN: 979-8-706175-50-4

For anyone in need of a little escapism

CHAPTER 1

I SHOULD HAVE arranged to meet Rose further up the road to walk into college together. Instead, I was waiting alone by the imposing wooden doors at the front entrance. I desperately tried to look calm and confident, whilst actually fighting an overwhelming feeling of nausea. Hundreds of students came bounding up the stone steps whilst chatting away animatedly. I had to move to the side to avoid being dragged along with the crowd. I pulled my phone out of my jeans pocket and pretended to be deep in thought composing a very important text message;

Hi Mum. First day at college going great so far. Every-one seems nice. See you later xx

The truth was I hadn't spoken to anyone yet. I'm not someone who makes friends easily. I need time to get to know and trust people. I guess I'm scared of being rejected. Again.

'Mollie! Hi! Over here!'

I glanced up from sending my very important text

message and saw a familiar hand waving in the air above the crowd. Rose's multi-coloured jumper was certainly a daring choice for our first day at college, but I wouldn't have expected anything less from her. Rose was my best friend all through secondary school. She was brave and/or stupid enough to befriend me after I had walked into our form room with toilet paper dragging from my shoe. Rose taught me how to laugh at myself, a skill which has turned out to be very useful and frequently utilised.

'Rose, I'm so glad you're here,' I said, giving her a big hug.

'I'm so excited, aren't you? So many new people to get to know,' Rose said as we ventured inside the bustling college.

'Uh yeah, super exciting.'

'And I'm so glad I don't have to study boring subjects like science and maths ever again.'

'Err, I'm studying science and maths!' I exclaimed.

'Oh yeah, sorry, no offence. I'm sure you'll have *loads* of fun!' Rose teased.

Despite getting on so well and being pretty much inseparable, myself and Rose have always had very different interests. Rose is impressively creative and has picked drama, dance and English language for her AS levels. I have chosen to study biology, chemistry, maths and PE. It seemed like a good idea at the time.

'Let's head to the great hall for the welcome talk,' I

suggested, to which Rose smiled and nodded her head.

The "great" hall was a less than accurate description. Nothing about the run down college was particularly great, least of all the multipurpose hall used for assemblies, meetings, music recitals and some sports. There was also a kind of musty smell hanging in the air. I hoped I might get used to that with time. Despite appearances it was the best ranked college in the area, so I was determined to stay open-minded.

I sat down next to Rose on one of the many red plastic chairs that lined the hall. Looking uncomfortable up on a podium at the front of the hall, the College Principal, Mr Golding, tapped his microphone and cleared his throat before starting his welcome speech. He was wearing an old-fashioned grey suit and a garish yellow tie. 'Whilst we are very keen for you to enjoy your time at Tanglewood College, you must be prepared to work hard to achieve your goals. You are college students now; you will not be spoon fed ...' He spoke in a monotonous voice and with a complete lack of enthusiasm which suggested he had given this speech a million times before.

Glancing around the hall at the hundreds of new students, it appeared everyone was keen to express themselves after years of having to comply with school uniforms of knee-length skirts and shapeless white shirts. The hall looked like a designer outlet store with the number of brands emblazoned across people's clothes. I suddenly felt self-conscious in my faded black skinny jeans and plain blue loose-fitting top.

I whispered in Rose's ear, 'Can we go clothes shopping this weekend? I feel very underdressed.'

'Sure we can,' Rose replied. 'But don't change your style for anyone else. I don't!'

I knew she was right, but it didn't make me feel any less insecure. I had always felt a bit invisible at school and I desperately wanted college to be different. All I wanted to do was make friends and fit in. It couldn't be that hard, surely?

Mr Golding was still droning on. 'I very much hope that you will all uphold the reputation that Tanglewood College has built over the years …'

I nudged Rose and pointed out a row of four girls with flawlessly styled hair and beautifully manicured nails. They were all pouting into their compact mirrors and applying lip gloss in perfect unison. We both stifled a laugh and Rose rolled her eyes. My shoulder-length mousey-brown hair and Rose's auburn waves were no match for those girls. I comforted myself with the knowledge of how low maintenance my hair is as it dries naturally straight. Sometimes I get bored with my hair colour and try out a home hair-dye kit, but not once has it ever turned out the glossy colour promised on the box.

Apparently, Mr Golding had finally finished his uninspiring speech as everyone started to stand and shove their way towards the exit.

'I guess this is it,' I said to Rose as we pushed our way

through the doors and back into the front foyer.

'You're going to be totally fine,' Rose said, giving me a big hug. She knew me too well and could clearly tell I was nervous. 'Good luck. I'll meet you in the canteen later for lunch,' Rose added as she headed off in search of the dance hall for her first lesson.

The campus was pretty big so the college had been kind enough to supply us with a map in our welcome packs. However, I was sure it must be out of date as I should have been standing outside my maths classroom yet was in fact standing next to an old basketball hoop on the edge of the campus. Having said that, my directional abilities are so incredibly poor I could get lost in my own back garden.

'Are you here for maths with Miss Hawkins too?' A guy with longish, sandy-blonde hair had suddenly appeared behind me. He was looking inquisitively at his map whilst constantly rotating it round in his hands, ninety degrees at a time.

'Oh, good. So I'm not the only one who can't read a map,' I said.

'I'm Matthew.' He smiled and extended his right arm.

'I'm Mollie. Nice to meet you.'

Usually I hate awkward handshakes. However, there was something very endearing about Matthew and he had a sort of rugged charm. His eyes were a dazzling sapphire blue, with dark lashes longer than mine even after two coats of mascara. I stared a second too long into his eyes and started to blush. I blush far too easily and as soon as I start to feel my face turn the tiniest bit pink, it escalates to full blown tomato at an alarming rate. Thankfully, Matthew didn't seem to notice and continued to rotate the map in his hands. Even with my limited navigational skills I didn't think holding it upside down and back to front was going to help.

'This way I reckon …' Matthew said as he confidently strode off in the direction of a particularly old looking part of the college. 'This seems like the kind of place they would hide us maths geeks.'

Hmm, I didn't really want to get labelled as a geek on my very first morning. College was meant to be the time to reinvent yourself and be whoever you wanted to be. Apparently that was easier said than done.

We somehow made it to the classroom (run-down old hut) with a minute to spare. Unsurprisingly, the only two seats left were at the very front. I slid down the row and pulled out a plastic chair next to a stern-looking girl who didn't even look up from her textbook. Matthew must have noticed too. 'I bet she sleeps with her calculator under her pillow,' he whispered in my ear. I suppressed a laugh as he sat down next to me.

'Okay everyone, settle down,' Miss Hawkins said. She was young and seemed enthusiastic, in stark contrast to Principal Golding. 'Incase you hadn't guessed, I'm Miss Hawkins. Well done for all finding your way here and high fives all round for choosing the best subject on the planet!'

Okay, maybe a little too enthusiastic.

'Firstly,' she continued, 'why shouldn't you let advanced maths intimidate you?' Her eyes scanned around the classroom and her red lips were already curling into a smile. 'Because it's really as easy as pi!'

Miss Hawkins chuckled to herself as she sat down on her swivelling desk chair, before looking up and realising no one else was laughing. I flashed her a sympathetic half-smile. Then she made us all go round the room and introduce ourselves with an "interesting fact", which I hate. It's so difficult to think of something that may genuinely interest people whilst not looking like you're showing off or just sounding plain weird. Of course, Miss Hawkins started at the front of the room so I was really under pressure.

The first guy proudly declared, 'I have done three sky dives.' Show off.

The girl next to him said, 'I have a collection of two hundred teddy bears.' Weird.

The stern-looking girl on my left surprised me with, 'I have three tattoos.' Interesting. I really need to learn not to judge a book by its cover.

My turn. 'I am deathly afraid of pigeons.'

Oh dear, the pressure had definitely got to me. 'It's the way they bob their heads and their beady little eyes,' I tried to explain.

People were laughing at me. I started to blush uncontrollably, my vision blurred, I felt disoriented and for a split second I felt as though I had no control over my own body. Despite all this I could faintly make out Matthew next to me saying, 'I'm deathly afraid of cats. Can't stand the creatures. They always look like they're plotting to kill you.' A couple of people behind us sniggered. I presumed from Matthew's crooked grin that he said that to take the attention away from me and I was very grateful. It gave me a chance to calm down and compose myself.

'Thank you,' I silently mouthed at Matthew.

'Any time,' Matthew replied with a wink.

After Miss Hawkins recapped some GCSE material and outlined the topics for the coming weeks, we were finally excused for lunch. I shoved my textbook and pens back into my brown shoulder bag and made my way to the door.

'Do you fancy taking a wander round campus to get our bearings?' Matthew asked me, his eyes wide and hopeful.

'Maybe later,' I said. 'I want to meet my friend for lunch first.'

'Okay. I hope there's no pigeon on the specials menu!'

Ha … ha. I shot Matthew a mock disapproving look as he walked away but I secretly liked his cheeky wit. He should help to make maths lessons slightly more bearable.

It took me a mere twenty minutes to locate the canteen. Oh, what I wouldn't give to have a decent sense of direction. The canteen was already filling up. The A-level students were all standing their ground in their favourite eating spots whilst the new intake tried to establish their place. I desperately wanted to find Rose and update her on my morning. We always told each other everything. I scanned the canteen from the safety of the door but there was no sign of Rose. I guessed she was still in her dance class. I made a mental note to ask her to teach me what she learns since I dance like I have two left feet.

I joined the long line for the food counter. The spaghetti bolognese looked nice but hardly practical for the first day of college. I opted for the safe option of a plate of chips. The diet can always start tomorrow. I also picked up a berry smoothie, as though that would offset the calories somehow. As I handed over the cash for my overpriced meal I glanced behind me to see where I might fit in. I saw a table of guys and girls wearing black leather jackets and sporting multiple piercings. I saw a table of sporty types, each person wearing at least three separate items of Nike branded clothing.

Then I spotted a table of girls who looked nice enough. I sat down on one of the spare seats and smiled nervously at the three girls on the other side of the table. No response. Well this is awkward. On closer inspection I think these girls might be second years and not interested in making a new, very ordinary girl like myself feel welcome on her first day. All three girls had long shiny hair and their makeup looked professionally applied. In comparison I suspected my cheap eyeliner was already halfway down my face.

I looked down and concentrated on my plate of chips but I couldn't help eavesdropping. The blonde girl in the middle was chatting away excitedly. Her friends couldn't get a word in as this girl talked without stopping for breath and her salad sat in front of her untouched. 'Do you think he still likes me? We haven't had much of a chance to talk yet. We kept in touch over the summer, obviously, but it was difficult as I was away in Italy a lot. But I'm sure we can pick up where we left off.'

'Hi, I'm Mollie,' I finally plucked up the courage to interrupt.

'And?' the girl in the middle replied. Her stare was intimidating and I immediately regretted saying anything.

'And, it's my first day here. Uh, of course it is. It's everyone's first day, sorry.'

'Not ours, we're second years.'

'Oh right, I did think you looked older.'

'Excuse me?'

'No, not old of course, just more, sophisticated?' I hoped that would appease them. 'So, what's good to eat here? The spaghetti bolognese looked nice?'

'We wouldn't know, we're vegetarian.'

'Oh, cool. I tried that once, but I just love bacon too much.' The three girls all just looked at me, completely repulsed, as though I had just slaughtered a pig right in front of them on the table.

I smiled apologetically and decided it would be best if I just stopped talking. I looked round the canteen searching desperately for Rose and at the same time I absent-mindedly tore open my sachet of ketchup. Does the company purposely make them near impossible to open?

'What the hell!' Suddenly the girl in the middle leapt to her feet and leaned across the table, glaring at me with almost bright-orange coloured eyes. I'm sure they had looked blue just moments earlier. Red sauce dripped from her white silk top as her friends tried to dab at it with napkins, inevitably making it worse.

'I'm … so …' was all I could seem to force out. I could feel my cheeks starting to burn and I felt dizzy and disoriented again. Everything looked blurred. I felt detached from my body and completely out of control.

'It's ruined! It's ruined!' was all I could make out through the ringing in my ears.

I was so grateful to feel a steadying hand on my shoulder and hear a familiar soothing voice.

'I'm so sorry about that. Can I offer you my scarf to wear to cover the stain?' Rose must have seen what happened and tried to make amends on my behalf.

'Seriously? I wouldn't be seen dead in that,' the girl sneered back, her eyes narrowed and her fists clenched.

'Be careful, you don't want to shift here,' I heard one

of the angry girl's friends whisper in her ear. Whatever that meant.

In perfect unison the three girls took a sharp intake of breath, turned on their heels and stomped off. I could feel people around us staring and I didn't know what to do or say but I looked up at Rose gratefully.

'Don't mention it,' she said. 'I've always got your back.'

CHAPTER 2

T HE REMAINDER OF my first day of college mostly
consisted of clock watching in biology. From
chromosomes to cytoplasm, from meiosis to mitochon-
dria. All I knew for sure was that my brain hurt and I
wanted to go home.

On the plus side, I had found myself seated next to an
attractive guy. The biology teacher, Mrs Flint, seemed
very strict so we hadn't dared chat to one another. But I
caught him looking over my shoulder at the cell diagrams
we had been instructed to label. He just smiled at me
unapologetically and continued to copy my answers.
Meanwhile, Mrs Flint wandered round the classroom,
checking on people's progress.

'Very good, Mollie,' Mrs Flint said as she passed.

'Thanks, Mum,' I replied. 'Uh, I mean, Mrs Flint.'

Argh. What is wrong with me? I just put my head
down on the table and tried to block out the sniggering
all around me.

Brrrrrring! The final bell could not have come early
enough. On top of everything else, I was worried about

the funny turns I had experienced today. I had never been particularly good in embarrassing or stressful situations, but I had never had a reaction as strong as that before where I felt completely out of control of my own body. I wondered whether I should book an appointment with my doctor, but it was such a strange sensation I wouldn't know how to even begin to explain it.

Rose and I had planned to walk home together and I waited for her in the same spot at the front of the college where I had met her that morning. It felt like a lifetime ago, not only seven hours. Rose bounded towards me down the corridor with a group of girls who were all smiling and talking animatedly. Rose looked really happy. And I was happy for her. Honestly. I just wish my college reinvention had gone a little smoother. Rose peeled herself off from the group and walked over to me.

'Let's get out of here,' she said with a smile, before waving goodbye to her new friends.

'Yes please,' I replied. I just wanted to get home, switch off and watch some trashy television.

'So, tell me all about your day,' Rose said as we made our way down the college steps.

'I think my performance at lunchtime overshadowed anything else that happened today.'

'Oh, don't worry about that, it will all be forgotten in a few days.' I appreciate the way Rose is always so supportive and reassuring, even though I'm pretty sure she realises those were not the kind of girls who will easily forgive and forget. With any luck I won't bump into them again.

'What will all be forgotten?' I heard a familiar voice behind me and felt a tap on my right shoulder. As I turned to look, Matthew appeared on my left side sporting his cheeky grin again. I couldn't help but smile back at him.

'Nothing,' I replied hastily whilst desperately trying not to look as flustered as I felt. 'Rose, this is Matthew from my maths class. Matthew, this is my best friend Rose.' They smiled at each other politely, then Rose turned to me and raised her eyebrows. I knew exactly what she was thinking and shot her a look straight back to say, '*Just play it cool*'.

'Are you two going to the Battle of the Bands night this weekend?' Matthew asked.

'Well, um, I ...' I had seen the posters advertising the event stuck all round college today and it looked fun; an evening of (attempting to) dance to various college bands and a good chance to meet new people. Unfortunately my mum has been very protective of me in recent years. Maybe it's because I'm an only child. Maybe it's because Dad inexplicably left us five years ago. Either way, I could already see that getting permission from Mum to go to the event was going to be a struggle.

'Definitely,' Rose cut in, giving me another look which I received as, '*Please act cool in front of this hot guy and sort things out with your over-bearing mother later*'.

Fortunately, Matthew seemed to have missed our interchange. 'Great, then I look forward to seeing you both there. It was nice to meet you, Rose. See you soon, maths geek,' he said as he gave me a wink with his beautiful blue eyes. Then he jogged on to join a group of guys walking ahead of us who all greeted him warmly with high fives.

'So,' Rose started. I already knew where this was going. 'When I asked how your day had been, you didn't think to mention your new hot maths geek friend?'

'He's not that hot,' I replied. I wasn't sure why I was being so defensive. I could feel my heart still fluttering in my chest so I couldn't lie to myself that he had no effect on me. No need for Rose to know that yet though. I had experienced plenty of crushes in the past and they had all been very much one-sided, so I didn't want to get my hopes up just yet.

We shortly arrived at Rose's house which she shared with her parents, her older brother Jake and their dog Milo, who came bounding outside wagging his tail as soon as Rose's dad opened the front door. Milo jumped up at me and I gave him a stroke behind his floppy ears.

'Milo, come back here,' Rose's dad shouted. 'Oh, hello, Mollie. How are you? I apologise for Milo's lack of respect for personal space.'

'It's fine, honestly, I love Milo. And I'm good, thanks.'

'Would you like to come in?' Rose's dad asked.

'Thanks, but I had better get home. Mum's made

lasagne and I expect she wants to interrogate me about my first day at college.'

Rose's dad smiled and nodded as he headed back inside.

'I'll see you in the morning Mollie,' Rose said as she entered her house, closely following by Milo.

I started the further ten-minute walk to my house. My pace quickened. I have a habit of always walking fast whether I'm in a hurry or not, plus I'm always on auto-pilot around this area as I have lived in Tanglewood all my life. It is a reasonably quiet neighbourhood without much excitement, although it's not too far from the bright lights of London. Some days I long to escape this predictable town but I wouldn't ever want to leave Mum on her own.

I passed by some woodland and something caught my attention. A rustling in the bushes. Then two flashes of light. Eyes? A crack of a twig. Then nothing. It had been a long day, I was probably just stressed and on edge.

I eventually arrived home to the two bedroom terraced house I shared with my mum. I can't deny sometimes I wish we had a little more space. I think we would argue less if we weren't under each other's feet so much. But I admire Mum and am so thankful to her for looking after me on her own after Dad left. He left when I was in my first year of secondary school. I came home from school one evening to find Mum crying hysterically clutching a piece of paper. Dad had left a short note saying he had to leave, he didn't know if, or when, he could return so we should forget about him and move on. He also wrote about how much he loved us. Ha! If that was the case, then he wouldn't have left in such a cowardly way with no real explanation. Mum assumes he was having an affair and her self-confidence has never recovered.

Our rusty gate squeaked as I pushed it open and it sent a black cat running out from under a nearby hedge. I bent down and stroked his soft fur. He was very friendly as usual and purred loudly as I scratched the top of his head. I didn't know where he lived but he looked well fed and groomed so I didn't feel too guilty leaving him outside as I stepped inside the front door.

'Good evening, sweetheart. How was your day?' Mum appeared immediately in the hallway as if she had been poised, waiting for me to return home. She had her spotty kitchen apron on and a tea towel slung over her shoulder.

'It was fine, thanks.' I yawned involuntarily. I didn't sleep well last night. I had laid in bed awake, running through hundreds of scenarios of things that could possibly go wrong on my first day of college. I would say my day had been about half as bad as I had imagined it could have been.

'You can tell me all about it over dinner.' Apparently Mum wasn't going to give up that easily.

I took a seat at our small wooden table whilst Mum pulled the lasagne out of the oven. It smelt amazing and looked big enough to feed a family of six. I often wondered if Mum wished she had a bigger family and if life would be a little easier if I had a brother or sister. I would love Mum to have more company, but she has only been on two dates since Dad left that I have known about, and the last one must have been a couple of years ago now. It's not something I tend to talk to her about, but I guess she must find it hard to trust men now.

'So, have you made lots of new friends?' Mum asked between mouthfuls of food.

'Everyone seems nice.' Except the girls I encountered at lunch time.

'Is there anyone you don't think you will get on with?' Mum doesn't miss a trick.

'No, not really,' I said. No need to relive today's trauma.

'Any handsome young men?'

'No, not really,' I repeated. I concentrated on my plate of food, hoping Mum wouldn't push any further. I hadn't made up my own mind exactly what I thought about Matthew yet.

'Oh, okay.' Mum also looked down at her plate. Fortunately, she felt just as awkward talking about boys as I did.

Right, I needed to cut to the chase. I took a deep breath and concentrated on making my voice sound as natural as possible, which ended up having the opposite effect. 'There's an event on at college this Saturday night.'

'What kind of event?' Mum asked, her eyes narrowing.

'It's Battle of the Bands night. Just a bit of music and dancing,' I said, before adding, 'Rose is allowed to go.'

'How many times do I have to tell you I don't care what other people are allowed to do?' Why does Mum insist on talking to me like I'm thirteen rather than sixteen? 'Will there be alcohol?' she continued.

'I don't think so.'

Mum looked at me, concern written all over her face. It struck me how she was starting to look older with more greying hair and deepening wrinkles. But she was definitely ageing gracefully and beautifully and I would be lucky to look as good as her when I am older.

'No, there will definitely be no alcohol,' I lied, as that was simply something I couldn't guarantee at a college event, and I think Mum knew that deep down.

'Okay, but I will drop you off and pick you up, no later than eleven o'clock.'

'It's okay, I can just walk with Rose,' I said.

'It's not safe for you two to be walking that late at night.'

'We'll be careful; we're not stupid,' I said sulkily.

'It's not you I don't trust, it's other people.'

Damn. That was Mum's answer to most things. I knew once she had pulled that line out there was no use arguing any further.

'Thanks, Mum.' I gathered up our used plates and

roughly stacked them in the dishwasher before heading upstairs to my bedroom.

I opened my bedroom door cautiously so as not to disturb the clothes that I had carefully laid out on the floor. Mum calls it my 'floor-drobe'. It infuriates her that I won't hang my clothes up in my perfectly good wardrobe and she will periodically come in and hang them all up for me. My desk, which Mum agreed to buy me before I started at college and foolishly thought I would use for coursework, is completely covered in make-up and hair accessories. Hidden behind my dry shampoo, which I couldn't live without, is a photo of Dad holding me as a baby. He's looking at me lovingly like I am his whole world. But he obviously didn't love me enough to want to stay. I have to hand it to him, he was a good actor. Right up until the day he left I thought we were a very happy family. He was the perfect dad really; spontaneous and fun, but also sensible and ready to give sound advice when needed. Plus, he and Mum always seemed so nauseatingly in love.

Knock knock.

Mum stuck her head round the door. I saw her looking at my floor-drobe in dismay and fighting the urge to scold me for the millionth time. She let out a small sigh before saying, 'I was thinking, I could pick you up from the party at midnight if you would like to stay for a bit longer?'

'That would be great Mum, if you're sure you don't

mind. Thank you.' We both smiled. I appreciated that she was trying to give me a bit more freedom and I knew it wasn't easy for her. 'Goodnight, Mum. Sleep well.'

CHAPTER 3

I DIDN'T SLEEP well at all and spent most of the early hours of the morning lying on my back staring at the ceiling. Eventually I forced myself out of my warm bed, took a long, hot shower and roughly blow-dried my hair. I brushed my eyelashes with mascara and dabbed concealer on my multiple spots. I looked in the mirror and decided all I had achieved was to make them more noticeable. In the end I had no time to eat breakfast so I grabbed a cereal bar to eat on the walk into college.

Mum caught me rushing out of the kitchen. 'Mollie! Aren't you going to eat something proper? I can make you some toast? Eggs? Bacon?'

'Thanks Mum, but I really don't want to be late to college.'

'Alright love, but be careful where you're walking. There's been an article in the local paper about a big cat sighting. Janet from book club told me about it and I didn't believe her at first, she's always exaggerating, but there's photographic proof, look …'

Mum shoved the paper under my nose. The photo

showed a big blurry shadow partially hidden by a tree. Hardly proof of there being a lion or tiger on the loose but I didn't have time to argue.

'I'll be careful, Mum. I promise,' I said as I hurried out the door.

Butterflies fluttered in my stomach as I power walked down the street and wondered what embarrassing situations I would get myself into today. I had to admit I was a little disappointed I didn't have maths today so I wouldn't get to see Matthew. But I did have my first PE lesson, which should be interesting.

I was panting by the time I reached the college gates and decided I needed to head straight to the toilets to touch up my make up that I had started to sweat off.

'Good morning, geek,' I heard a voice behind me. Of course, perfect timing to bump into Matthew, who looked effortlessly cool as usual.

'Good morning,' I said breathlessly, feeling very self-conscious. Matthew didn't seem to notice.

'How's your timetable looking today?' he asked.

'I've got double PE this morning.'

'Ah, good luck with that. I've heard Mr Armstrong doesn't take any prisoners.' Matthew smiled but this news filled me with fear.

'Oh dear, I knew I should have kept my fitness up over the summer. I hope I can keep up.' I forced a smile back through my panic. I never thought I would be the top of my PE class but I hoped I wouldn't be completely useless.

'You'll be fine,' Matthew said. He looked directly at me with his beautiful blue eyes and instantly I could feel my nerves settling. 'See you later, hopefully. We could work on the maths homework together?'

'You mean you need my help?' I teased.

'Ah, you see straight through me!' And with that Matthew strolled away and I was free to dart to the toilets to check my face.

I pushed open the horribly bright pink toilet door (pink for girls, how original) and immediately saw the three girls whom I had had a run-in with at lunch yesterday. They were all lined up along the mirror staring at their reflections intensely and adding more makeup to their already perfectly made-up faces.

I was not in the mood this morning for another confrontation with them. I thought about turning around and dashing straight back out. But no, that was pathetic, I was sure they didn't all hate me. They'd probably forgotten all about it by now.

The evil eyes I received from all of them, in impressively perfect synchronisation, and the hushed whispering, suggested otherwise.

I pretended I hadn't noticed and rushed into the nearest cubicle, slamming the door behind me. Instead of fighting for space at the mirror with the other girls I decided to just dab at my undoubtedly shiny face with some toilet roll and ran a finger under each eye to wipe away any smudged eyeliner. That was going to have to do. I could overhear the girls' conversation.

'Amber, have you decided on your outfit for Saturday yet?'

Amber must be the ringleader whose top I accidentally ruined.

'No, we should go clothes shopping after college. I need to look amazing to show a certain someone what he's been missing,' Amber replied.

'Do you think he will actually commit to being your boyfriend this year?' I sensed Amber's friend had pushed her luck as Amber took a couple of seconds to reply.

'I don't know, but what else can I do? I know he can be a bit arrogant and thoughtless sometimes, but then when we're alone he shows his softer side and I just can't resist.'

As they continued to gossip I took the opportunity to sneak out of the bathroom undetected. I sighed with relief as I scurried away.

We had been told to meet outside the changing rooms for our first PE lesson. Fortunately it was easier to find than it had been to find my maths class. A tall man, probably in his thirties, was standing outside the changing rooms. He had his arms folded across his chest and his muscles bulged through his thin, tight white T-shirt. A referee's whistle hung loosely around his neck. There was no mistaking this must be the PE teacher, Mr Armstrong.

'Very apt,' I thought.

'I'm sorry?'

Uh oh, did I say that out loud?

'Name?' Mr Armstrong asked sternly in a deep voice.

'Err, Mollie Thomas.'

Mr Armstrong nodded towards the female changing room. 'Well, Err Mollie Thomas, be ready for rounders in ten minutes on the sports field.'

My mouth had turned too dry to reply so I put my head down and snuck past him into the changing room.

Oh the joys of communal changing rooms! Especially awkward when you don't know anyone. Plus to add to my anxiety, practical PE lessons were mixed first and second years to make up the numbers to be able to play proper matches. I found a quiet corner and pulled out my loose-fitting black shorts, plain round-neck T-shirt and muddied trainers. I had always gone for comfort and practicality over fashion when it came to sport. Perhaps something I was starting to regret as I glanced up to see girls squeezing into tight branded leggings and equally fitted and stylish T-shirts.

Not wanting to be the last one out, I grabbed a hair-band from my bag and scraped my hair up into a messy ponytail as I walked out onto the sports field. There were around fifteen people already on the field and most of the girls were already stretching (posing). A couple of metres away all the guys were kicking a football around in a circle. I presumed this was more than a mere game of keepy-uppy and in fact a ritual to determine who the alpha male in the group was going to be.

One of the guys kicked the ball too hard (definitely out of the running for alpha male) and it started to roll towards me. Chasing after the ball was the most gorgeous guy I have ever seen. Tall, dark and handsome personified. He looked older than sixteen. Just the right amount of muscles. Strong eyebrows framing beautiful green eyes. Dark brown hair just long enough to bounce around his face as he ran. And the most kissable looking lips.

Wow, those lips.

Uh oh. He stopped jogging and stood a few metres away with his hands on his hips, panting slightly. The ball came to a stop at my feet. He raised a perfect hand and waved with a smile. My legs turned to jelly. Not helpful, given the fact I presumed he wanted me to kick the ball back to him. I waved and smiled back, perhaps a little overzealously, and swung my right leg back whilst praying my foot would make contact with the ball. My prayers were answered as I struck the ball flawlessly. At that exact moment Amber ran past me from behind, her long blonde flowing ponytail blowing in the wind. She ran straight up to my perfect guy, flung her arms around his neck and wrapped her legs around his waist. He twirled her round and planted a kiss on her cheek. Meanwhile my perfectly passed ball rolled just behind his feet towards the rest of the guys who looked at me pityingly.

Fortunately, at that point, Mr Armstrong strode onto the field so everyone quietened and Amber unwrapped herself from Mr tall, dark and handsome.

'Welcome to physical education. This isn't going to be the easy option some of you may have thought it would be. So if there is anyone here who is not ready to work hard and give me one hundred and ten percent effort, you can leave now.'

Wow, what a warm welcome. I wonder if he's always so serious. As I glanced around I could see people shuffling awkwardly and looking down at their trainers but no one left.

'Right, let's get straight into a game of rounders; see what you're all made of. Line up in height order. Girls this side, boys this side.'

No one dared say a word as we all scuttled into position. I was one of the tallest girls, although I didn't see how that would be any advantage in rounders.

'One, two, one, two, one, two…' Mr Armstrong barked as he strode down the line.

The teams started to congregate. It was obvious Amber's group had arranged themselves so they would be on the same team. I said a silent prayer I wouldn't be with them.

'Two.' Phew.

I walked over to my team and saw Mr tall dark and handsome there, already taking the lead and giving everyone fielding positions. I heard one of the other guys call him Jamie.

'And who wants to go on fourth base?' Jamie asked. 'How about you?'

Was he looking at me with his piercing green eyes?

'Uh …' was all that came out. Jamie must have taken that as a yes as he declared, 'Great, let's go,' and then he initiated a team chant.

Our team were up to bat first. Jamie of course took the lead and opened up the scoring with a rounder. I noticed Amber squeal in delight and jump up and down in her tiny shorts, despite being on the other team. Jamie ran down the line, high fiving all of us standing in line waiting to bat. I smiled at him and tried to make eye contact but he barely noticed me as he carried on down the line.

As I stepped up to bat, my aim wasn't to get a rounder but to merely make contact with the ball. I tried to concentrate on the ball as it was released from the bowlers hands but I could see Amber out of the corner of my eye with her hands poised, hoping to catch me out. I managed to hit the ball just far enough to allow me to reach first base. I let out a sigh of relief.

My team ended on fourteen rounders, mainly thanks to Jamie. We then took up our fielding positions. Jamie had put himself as a deep fielder, presumably because his muscular arms gave him an impressive throw.

The other team started racking up the rounders from the outset. However, Jamie's impressive fielding kept us in the game. We managed to get a couple of people out at first base whose batting turned out to be even worse than mine. I wasn't doing too badly and had only missed a couple of catches.

The score was fourteen to thirteen and Amber was the last person left to bat. She strutted confidently up to the spot, swinging the bat round in her hand and I couldn't help but admire her perfectly toned legs. The boys were heckling her but that didn't stop her from striking the ball flawlessly into the outfield. She gave a girly squeal and did a little jump which somewhat detracted from the good hit, but then she started to run. Jamie was chasing after the ball with impressive speed and quickly bent to pick it up. I was transfixed watching him run.

'Melanie, heads up, Melanie!'

I continued to stare at Jamie, bemused. Uh oh, he was talking to me. Jamie had launched the ball into the air and it was hurtling towards me. I had to make the catch for us to win the game. I put my arms in the air and willed the ball into my hands before Amber made it all the way round.

And then, all of a sudden, everything went black.

CHAPTER 4

I DON'T THINK I was out for long but I slowly opened my eyes to find a concerned, fuzzy face staring down at me. After blinking a couple of times, I realised it was Matthew.

'You've already got a massive bump on your head,' he said with a gentle smile. I put my hand to my bruised forehead and winced in pain.

'I'm fine,' I insisted whilst sitting up and immediately realising I in fact wasn't. Matthew helped me to my feet and put a supportive arm around my back. I felt safe in his arms but also weak and embarrassed. I saw Jamie walking away and chatting with Amber ahead of us. He hadn't bothered to say sorry or even check I was alive.

'Let me walk you home,' Matthew said, with a look of concern in his eyes.

'Don't be silly, I can walk by myself. Besides I have more classes this afternoon.'

Matthew grinned knowingly as he pulled his arm away from me and watched for a second. I swayed and staggered before he caught me again softly in his arms.

'Fine, I give in, you win,' I said managing a half-smile which increased the throbbing pain in my head. I paused before adding, 'I don't like asking for help.'

'You didn't ask, I offered. Insisted even! I'm not doing it out of the goodness of my heart anyway, I'm planning to make you do my maths homework for the rest of the month.'

'And there I was thinking you were just being nice! You don't need my help with maths anyway; you're pretty good.'

'Wow, a compliment. Your head injury must be worse than I thought … we had better get you to the hospital, quick!' Matthew said.

'Shut up,' I laughed.

'Actually, I have a confession.' Matthew's tone had become more serious. 'I've done the class before. I'm actually a second year but I'm resitting maths. I'm sorry I didn't tell you bcfore, I guess I was just a bit embarrassed.'

'Don't be silly, there's no need to be embarrassed. The way I'm going, I'll probably need to resit all my classes.'

As we walked (staggered) down my driveway Matthew said, 'I didn't think I would be meeting your parents so soon!'

'It's just my mum,' I said as she pulled open the door on cue.

'Mollie! Are you okay? What happened to you? I'll see if we've got any peas in the freezer…' Mum turned around and scurried back into the house. She hadn't even acknowledged Matthew. I looked up at him apologetically.

Once inside, I guided Matthew towards the living room and we sat down on the faded blue sofa. Mum came back from the kitchen carrying a bag of frozen carrots; I guessed that meant we were all out of peas.

'Let me take a look,' Mum said whilst inspecting my battle wounds. I flinched as she applied the frozen carrots to my forehead.

'I'll be fine, Mum. I just decided to catch the rounders ball with my head.'

'Well, thank you for taking care of my clumsy daughter,' Mum said with a smile, looking at Matthew.

'It's no trouble,' Matthew replied.

'I'm going to go upstairs and lie down,' I said wearily. Matthew walked behind me going up the stairs, poised to catch me incase I lost my balance. I was desperately praying that I hadn't left too many clothes lying on the floor. I opened my door and quickly bent down to scoop some stray socks into my washing basket. That caused my head to start spinning again so I flopped down on my bed and closed my eyes. The spinning slowed a little. I felt Matthew sit on the edge of my bed and could sense he was looking at me. I would usually feel really awkward but for some reason I felt safe with Matthew.

'You had better get well before Battle of the Bands this weekend,' Matthew said softly.

'I will, I promise. Thanks so much for walking me home, but you don't have to stay.' I secretly hoped that he would stay a little longer, but I also realised I wasn't at my most attractive with a bag of frozen carrots stuck on my head.

'It was my pleasure. Honestly.' With a wink he turned and walked down the stairs. The wink made me feel woozy … or maybe that was just the head injury.

That night I dreamt about the whole embarrassing scenario all over again. Only, in my dream it was Jamie that scooped me up in his strong arms and carried me home.

The rest of my week was pretty unremarkable in comparison. I continued to suck in PE classes, Matthew and I continued to get told off for chatting in maths class, and Rose and I continued to meet in the canteen for our lunchtime catch-ups.

Everyone was talking about the Battle of the Bands night. The girls were worrying about what to wear and the boys were plotting how they could sneak in alcohol. There were posters up all around college that the bands had made themselves. I always lingered a little whenever I walked past Jamie's poster for his band "Big Cats on Campus". One morning whilst I was staring a little too hard at Jamie's poster, I was distracted by a familiar voice.

'Hey, Mollie!' Rose shouted as she bounded towards me with one of her dance friends. Her friend was tall and beautiful, and walked with a poise and elegance which immediately gave away her dance background. 'This is Jenny. We just had a free period so we've been working on a secret handshake. It's for the dance group, but you can be an honorary member. Watch this.'

It was the most complex secret handshake I had ever seen. Rose and Jenny linked arms, spun each other round and bumped hips, among other moves I couldn't even describe. In the middle of their routine I noticed Amber and her friends walk past. They didn't look impressed and Amber made an "L" sign against her forehead, although ironically it was the wrong way round.

'Thanks, Rose,' I interrupted. 'I think I've got it.'

Rose followed my gaze towards Amber and her friends. 'Do you really care what they think?' she asked. 'You and I have always had a secret handshake.'

'But Rose, that was secondary school. We're at college now.'

'And now all you want to do is impress the popular girls? The ones that were mean to you on your first day, remember?'

'I can't explain it, but there's something about Amber I'm drawn to. And maybe I do want to be popular for once. Is that so wrong?'

'I just didn't realise you were so bothered by other people's opinions but that's fine, I'm so sorry I embarrassed you. Come on, Jenny. Let's go.'

'It was nice to meet you,' Jenny said awkwardly as Rose dragged her away.

I knew deep down I was being a bit unreasonable and I didn't want to hurt Rose, but I couldn't help how I felt.

Thankfully, Rose had forgiven me by the time the much anticipated Battle of the Bands night arrived. She came over to my house in the early evening to get ready. We had already planned to arrive at the event fashionably late.

Mum kept trying to be a good hostess by bringing us crisps, pizza and smoothies (she was determined that the smoothie maker she bought on a whim because "it was such a good deal" would not go to waste). No alcohol though, despite me insisting that everyone would be allowed at least one drink at home. '*Not until you're 18*'. I let Rose eat most of the food as I was starting to feel nauseous about having to dance in public.

'Pineapples or flamingos?' Rose asked whilst holding two funky dresses up to her enviably petite frame.

'Err, flamingos. Little black dress number one or little black dress number two?' I joked, holding up two almost identical dresses. I had many more similar in my wardrobe. I was already pretty set on dress number two so hoped Rose would agree.

Apparently Rose didn't approve of either as she said, 'Don't take this the wrong way, but I thought college was the time to experiment with your style?'

'I've got a new necklace I could wear with it? Besides, the little black dress is a classic.'

Rose said sheepishly, 'Well I actually brought you one

of my dresses to borrow. You can't say no until you try it on.'

Rose made me close my eyes as she slipped the silky dress on over my head. I felt like I was on a makeover show.

'Now open your eyes,' Rose said excitedly.

I stood in front of my mirror and slowly opened my eyes for the big reveal. I didn't recognise myself at first. I looked older and more mature, in a midnight blue silk dress with spaghetti straps. It was fitted around the body then hung loosely to my knees.

'I've never seen you wear this Rose?'

'Well actually, the thing is, it's my mum's …' Seeing my expression she hastily added, 'But it'll be totally fine. She never even wears it.'

'But I can't …' I stopped mid-sentence because I did really like the dress and I wanted to make a good impression at our first college event. Plus, Rose was right, her mum would never have to know.

Rose also wanted to give me a full face of make-up. She was used to doing it for her dance shows. However, I drew the line at mascara, a slick of pink lipstick and a dab of bronzer.

'Beautiful,' Rose said as she stepped back to admire her creation. 'Matthew won't be able to resist!'

I blushed. Matthew did have a certain charm but what I didn't tell Rose was that I was secretly looking forward to watching Jamie perform with his band. I was too infatuated currently to be told the truth – that I didn't stand a chance with him.

I took one last look in the mirror and smoothed down my dress. 'Let's go and enjoy our first ever college party!' I said.

'It's going to be great,' Rose declared as we tottered downstairs in our heels.

Mum was waiting in the hallway. 'Ah, look at you both, all grown up. Can I take a photo? Smile, Mollie! Now have you got enough money? And you're taking your phone? Remember, I'll be there at midnight to pick you up, but just ring me if you want to come home any earlier.'

'Yes, Mum.' I knew she would be worrying all evening until I was safely tucked up in my bed.

'Thanks, Mrs Thomas,' Rose said as we left the house. 'I promise I'll look after her, don't worry!'

The event was being held in the same "great hall" where we had our introductory lecture. The student organisers had done their best by draping some dark-blue fabric across the ceiling and blowing up what seemed like hundreds of blue and silver balloons. A stage had been constructed at the back of the hall and one of the student bands "Dragon Blood" were already playing. Despite their interesting choice of name, they actually weren't bad. Not that my taste in music is much to go by.

A group of Rose's dance friends, led by Jenny, came bounding over and gave her a hug. Rose gave me some awkward introductions but the music was too loud to hear any of their names so I just nodded and smiled. I envied all of their toned bodies and the way they effortlessly swayed along to the music. I tried (and failed) to copy them.

Suddenly I was being dragged towards the centre of the dance floor. I shook my head at Rose in a silent protest as she grabbed me round the wrist and pulled me through the crowd of students, but I knew she wouldn't take no for an answer. I did some awkward swaying movements for half a song before I took my chance to worm my way back to the safety of the edge of the dance floor. I headed towards the drinks table, where there were soft drinks only, of course. Although, despite the no-alcohol policy, I had already spotted at least ten people with hip flasks and there was a good chance the punch had been spiked, at least once.

'Hi, geek!' Matthew suddenly appeared beside me at the drinks table. He looked me up and down. 'You scrub up well!'

'I wish I could say the same,' I replied with a grin. Matthew did in fact look good in a simple grey T-shirt, dark jeans and messy hair. 'Thanks again for coming to my rescue the other day.'

'No problem. So, we have established rounders really isn't your sport. So, what is?'

'Well, I am slightly more coordinated when it comes to netball or basketball.'

'Cool, maybe I could take you on at some one-on-one basketball sometime?'

Was Matthew flirting with me? He was probably just being friendly, or maybe I really did look alright in Rose's mum's dress! I blushed and felt a tingle of electricity run down my spine. I hoped I wasn't going to have another funny episode; I never did get round to ringing the doctor's surgery.

Matthew broke the tension and said, 'That's okay, we'll let you get over your head injury first! I'm really sorry, I've got to run, I'm helping out backstage.'

'Ooh, that sounds fun, hanging out with the bands.'

'Nah, it's not so glamorous. Us roadies mostly just get bossed about.'

'Do you work with "Big Cats on Campus"?' I asked whilst trying to sound casual.

'You mean, do I work with Jamie?'

I shrugged sheepishly.

'I don't understand what everyone sees in him,' Matthew exclaimed. 'I mean sure, I can appreciate he's not a bad looking guy, but to be honest Mollie he knows that too. He can be pretty arrogant at times.'

I scowled. I wasn't ready to hear negative things about Jamie, who I had built up to be completely perfect in my head. 'Well it doesn't matter because there's no way he would be interested in me anyway.'

'Look, he's not a bad guy. We were thrown together due to a certain, um, situation and he was very support-

ive. But trust me, you can do so much better than him.'
Matthew paused for a second then added, 'You really do
look great Mollie. Oh, and watch out for the punch. It's
definitely been spiked.'

Once again I could feel heat rising from my neck into
my face accompanied by a tingling sensation down my
arms. Luckily, Matthew was already weaving through the
crowds, making his way backstage. It seemed like a good
time for a quick bathroom break and a check that I didn't
have any lipstick on my teeth.

As I entered the bathroom, unsurprisingly, Amber
and her friends were already occupying the mirror.
Amber looked so elegant in a figure-hugging black dress
that I immediately felt frumpy. I slid into a toilet cubicle,
hoping to go unnoticed.

There was much giggling and hushed whispering
between Amber and her friends but then it all went quiet.
Thinking that this was my chance to escape, I stepped out
of the cubicle … only to come face to face with Amber.

Amber was smiling. Was she smiling at me? I made
my way to the sinks and concentrated on furiously
soaping my hands. But then there was a gentle hand on
my back and Amber addressed me in the mirror.

'Mollie, it's so nice to see you. I hope your head's
better?'

I was surprised she knew my name. And that she
cared. 'Um, yes, it's fine. Thank you for asking.'

Amber still had her hand on my back and I felt a

strong urge to shrug it off.

'You look fab, by the way,' she said. 'Your dress is gorgeous. It makes you look far thinner.' Does she really think I can't recognise a backhanded compliment when it smacks me round the face?

I smiled politely and turned to leave.

'Hey, why don't you stay and have a drink with us?' Amber called out.

I looked around and saw her friends were each holding silver hip flasks encrusted with pink diamante.

'It's only vodka. Just try a bit,' one of Amber's friends said.

My immediate reaction was to politely decline and walk out. But then I remembered that once I stepped outside the bathroom I would have to venture back on to the dance floor. Maybe a sip of vodka would help me to loosen up a little.

'Sure.' I heard the word come out of my mouth before my brain had really weighed up the decision.

I reached out and took a hip flask from one of Amber's friends. They all looked at me expectantly. As I unscrewed the cap, the distinctive smell of vodka hit me before I had even put it to my lips.

'Bottoms up,' Amber said, chinking her hip flask against mine.

'Eurgh!' I couldn't help but pull a face as the vodka burned the back of my throat. 'Thanks very much,' I croaked, handing the flask back to Amber's friend. How do people drink that stuff?

'You have to drink more than that,' Amber said. 'Go ahead. Finish it.'

There was a mild threat in her voice. I don't know if it was because I wanted to impress her or because I just wanted to get out of the bathroom, but I drank the entire contents of the hip flask in one go. And I felt … fine. Surprisingly fine.

'Have a good night,' Amber called as I walked out of the bathroom.

The dance floor looked even more crowded and the bass guitar riffs vibrated around the hall. I went over to the edge of the dance floor and stood on tiptoes, trying to locate Rose. People kept shoving past me and spilling their drinks down my dress. I would have to get it dry cleaned before Rose returned it to her mum's closet.

I spotted Jamie standing alone by the drinks table pouring himself a large plastic cup of the spiked punch. My heart thumped in my chest. This was my chance. I sauntered over confidently.

'Heeey Mr Big Cat on Campus!' I pretty much shouted in his face.

'Um, hi, do I know you?' Jamie asked before downing his punch.

'Sorry, you probably don't recognise me out of my PE kit. I'm actually wearing my friend's mum's dress.'

'Okaaay,' he said, whilst turning to pour another cup of punch.

'Anyway, you threw the ball at my head in rounders …'

'Ah, you're the girl who needs to learn to catch with her hands together. Do it now, put your hands out in front of you as though you're about to catch.' I did as I was told, even though I was starting to feel a little dizzy. 'And this is where they should be, if you want to avoid being hit on the head again.' He pushed my hands together with his. My head was actually spinning now and I couldn't get any words out so I just gawped at him. *Say something Mollie! Anything!*

'Anyway, see you around, Melanie,' he said as he walked away, looking a little uncomfortable.

'It's Mollie!' I called after him feebly.

I felt a sudden rush of blood to the head and the music seemed to get even louder. Once I had steadied myself, I spotted Rose in the middle of the dance floor. What the heck, I should join her. I pushed my way through the crowd. I could tell I was annoying people by accidentally bumping into them. I couldn't help it, my balance was a little off. I found Rose's group and joined in the dancing. I definitely looked as good as they did, maybe even better.

'Hey, Rose, this is brilliant!' I shouted in her ear. She smiled and nodded, although I wasn't convinced she had heard me. 'I love you,' I exclaimed whilst giving her a hug which nearly resulted in both of us falling on the floor. I carried on dancing and the music continued to pound louder in my ears and the floor swayed in time with the music. All of a sudden, I felt a rise in my throat. And nausea. So much nausea.

'Excuse me,' I mumbled with my hand over my mouth, pushing my way off the dance floor. I knew I had knocked several people's drinks out of their hands to the floor but I needed to get back to the bathroom. Fast. Luckily Amber was still there and she held open the door for me. But I couldn't make it to a cubicle before I was sick all over the bathroom floor ... and someone's black leather shoe? Uh oh. I wiped my mouth with the back of my hand and slowly lifted my throbbing head. They didn't look like girls' shoes, or girls' trousers, or ... Oh no. I was looking up at Jamie's gorgeous face. In the men's toilet.

Jamie looked horrified. I could hear Amber sniggering by the doorway.

'Look what you've done. I have to perform in ten minutes,' Jamie growled.

'I ... I ...' Even if I knew what I wanted to say I still had too much vodka circulating in my bloodstream to get the words out.

Although I was dizzy and could barely see or think straight, I still felt mortified. My hands and feet started tingling and my face and neck felt like they were on fire. My vision must have been bad because when I looked down at my hands, they appeared to be changing shape. I tried to get up but my knees started to buckle and I felt Jamie's strong arms catch me. When I looked up at him this time, he looked alarmed and concerned and reassuringly less angry.

'Listen to me,' he said. 'You need to relax. Everything's going to be fine but I need to get you home.'

I think I let out a very weak protest before Jamie scooped me up in his arms and I passed out on his shoulder.

CHAPTER 5

I WOKE UP in my warm cosy bed, just like every other morning. But unlike every other morning my head was pounding, my mouth was as dry as a desert and … was that Mum sitting on the chair in the corner of my room?

'Never in my life have I been more disappointed in you, Mollie. For you to be in such a state you had to be carried home by a young man. I've sat here all night just to make sure you were still breathing. What on earth were—'

'I'm sorry Mum,' I interrupted, my voice hoarse and croaky. It was all coming back to me and there was nothing she possibly could say to make me feel any worse.

'Mollie, how many times have I taught you how to look after yourself? How many times have I tried to protect you from getting hurt? How many times have you promised me not to do anything stupid?'

I knew these were rhetorical questions so I remained silent. Plus, I was too dazed to form any kind of sentence.

I'm not sure how long I lay listening to Mum's lecture for before I fell back into a comatose sleep.

I spent the rest of the day feeling sorry for myself and trying to be extra nice to Mum. I even cooked dinner and did the washing up afterwards. Despite seeming angry, I knew that Mum was just worried about me. I think some of her anxieties stem from Dad abandoning us, which I can understand.

Mum silently picked up a tea towel to help me with the washing up. We hadn't spoken much during the day as I had been holed up in my room feeling hungover and regretful. 'I really am sorry Mum,' I said.

'I know you are, Mollie,' Mum sighed. 'It's just so unlike you. Did someone pressure you to drink? Did you feel you had to do it to fit in?'

'Kind of,' I replied, not looking up from the washing up bowl. 'How did you know?'

'Because, believe it or not, I remember what it was like to be a teenage girl. I had a few wild years before I met your dad, you know. But I wasted a lot of time and I didn't concentrate enough on my education. I don't want you to make the same mistakes as I did. But I do appreciate that you have so many more pressures on you now than I did in my day.'

'I don't believe you were ever "wild"!' I laughed. 'Thanks for being understanding, though. Does this mean I'm not grounded?'

'Oh no, I'm afraid you are still very much grounded,'

Mum said as she poured herself a glass of red wine and left me to finish the washing up.

Oh well, it was worth a try.

Mum wouldn't let Rose come round to the house on Sunday so I had to make do with a phone call, which I made from under my duvet in case Mum was trying to listen in.

'I don't think the *whole* college knows what happened,' Rose tried to console me, but I could hear the doubt in her voice.

'I'm never drinking again! Jamie must hate me, I feel so bad for ruining his shoes and making him miss his set.'

'He didn't miss his set; the "Big Cats on Campus" still played. He must have sprinted back from your house at superhuman speed to make it in time and he did look a little dishevelled, but he was still hot!'

'Oh, okay. Well that's good at least. I've got PE with him first thing tomorrow morning.'

'Are you going to talk to him?' Rose asked.

'No way, I'm too embarrassed. It's a big group, I can just stay out of his way.'

FAMOUS LAST WORDS. Monday morning came around far too quickly and I found myself standing in the college sports hall in my unflattering gym kit. I wasn't completely over my hangover and Mr Armstrong's booming voice and the harsh sports hall lights were giving me a headache. The college day had only just started but it was immediately clear to me that the *whole* college had either seen or heard about Saturday night's events. One group of guys had even made fake retching noises as I walked past. The saving grace of the day was that we were playing basketball in PE. Finally, a sport I wasn't completely useless at.

'Now, get into pairs for passing drills,' Mr Armstrong ordered.

I had made sure to stand as far away from Jamie and Amber as possible. But as I looked up to see if anyone else was partner-less, Jamie threw a basketball at my chest (which fortunately I caught) and he gestured for me to follow him into a corner of the sports hall. I followed obediently and out of the corner of my eye I caught Amber looking as surprised as I felt.

'Chest passes, shoulder passes and bounce passes,' came more orders from Mr Armstrong. 'Don't rush them. I want to see good technique.'

Jamie and I started to pass the ball back and forth in silence. I concentrated hard on making perfect passes, whilst it seemed no effort at all for Jamie.

Eventually, Jamie broke the silence. 'You're not bad at passing, Mollie. And I much prefer you throwing a ball at me to throwing up on me.'

I couldn't tell by his expression whether or not he was joking. 'I'm so sorry. Let me buy you some new shoes?'

'No need, they were old anyway. These things happen … although you do seem more disaster prone than most.'

'Yeah, it hasn't been the ideal start to college life, but I guess things can only get better!'

Jamie stopped passing the ball suddenly and stared directly into my eyes. I couldn't have looked away even if I wanted to. He looked like he was trying to figure something out, although I couldn't even begin to guess what.

'Come to korfball training this evening,' Jamie eventually said.

'What-ball?' I asked.

'Korfball. It's like basketball but better. I'd like you to try out.'

How could I say no when he continued to look at me with those piercing green eyes?

Before I could answer, Mr Armstrong blew his whistle unnecessarily loudly to gather everyone back in a group and change the drill.

Jamie whispered in my ear before we joined the group. 'Five thirty in this sports hall. What you're wearing will be fine.'

We ended up on different teams for the rest of the session, but I couldn't help replaying our conversation over and over in my head. Why was he suddenly showing an interest in me, especially after what I did? I was as confused as I was intrigued and excited.

I had maths class in the afternoon but I just couldn't

get my brain to focus on the equations. As usual, Matthew and I had whispered conversations whenever Miss Hawkins turned to write on the board. I excitedly told him my news. 'The strangest thing happened this morning ... Jamie was actually nice to me and then he invited me to korfball training.'

This was the first time I had ever seen Matthew lost for words. 'Oh. Um, right. I play korfball too. Do you know why he asked you to go?'

'Well, I can only presume because of my awesome basketball skills I showed him this morning.'

Matthew remained stony-faced. I was beginning to feel offended that he was so surprised I had been invited along.

Matthew must have sensed my annoyance. 'Look, it's just, Jamie's usually quite selective with who he invites to training. But I guess we'll just have to see how you get on this evening.'

I didn't reply because Miss Hawkins had turned around and glared at us disapprovingly. I wouldn't have known what to say to him anyway, although I think the look on my face expressed my irritation.

'And so x=?' Miss Hawkins looked at me and Matthew expectantly. I hadn't been listening to a word she had said. I glanced at the whiteboard and tried to do some quick mental arithmetic.

'One hundred and four?' I guessed.

'Not even close,' Miss Hawkins said with a sigh. 'I

know that budding new relationships are very exciting. I was your age once upon a time believe it or not. But if you two put as much effort into your work as you do talking then you might just pass the year.'

'Oh, it's not … I mean, we're not …' I said before I realised I was just making it worse and stopped talking. Matthew just buried his head in his textbook and we barely spoke for the rest of the lesson.

At the end of a long, mentally and physically tiring day, I went to meet Rose at the front of college as planned to walk home together. She was wearing her usual colourful clothes so was easy to pick out from the crowd.

'Hey, Rose. Thanks for waiting but I'm really sorry, I've had a change of plans. I'm trying out for the korfball team this evening.'

'The what team?'

I laughed. 'I know. I will explain everything tomorrow, I promise, but I won't be able to walk home with you tonight. Is that okay?'

'Of course it is; whatever you need to do. Good luck, break a leg,' Rose joked and waved me off with a smile.

I made my way back through the now eerily quiet corridors towards the changing rooms. I felt a knot forming in my stomach despite my best attempts to tell myself everything would be fine. What if I did actually break a leg? Not completely implausible given my recent luck, plus I had no idea what this sport even was. And Matthew had seemed less than keen about me going along.

Despite my reservations, I found myself in the changing room putting my unflattering and now less than fresh sports kit back on. I was surprised I was alone but checked my phone and realised it was nearly time for the start of the session. The others must already be in the sports hall. I walked up to the big double swinging doors and peered through the dirty window. It seemed to be pitch-black inside. Had I got the wrong time? Why did I mess everything up? But then I heard voices from inside.

'I wonder what she'll turn into.'

'Some kind of rodent, most likely.'

'Jamie could be wrong. Maybe she's not one of us.'

What on earth were they talking about? It sounded like complete gibberish. Perhaps I had misheard. I pushed my ear against the window so I could hear better but as I did so the door swung open and I ended up stumbling into the sports hall. As my eyes adjusted to the darkness I could just make out the shapes of around ten people sitting on benches on the other side of the hall. Nobody moved or spoke. This was a very odd training session. Then out of the corner of my eye, over my left shoulder, I was sure I saw two small flashes of light. Then they reappeared on my right. No, not flashes of light. Eyes. Two bright green piercing eyes half a metre from the ground. Approaching. Fast.

It couldn't be … Was that a panther? I was rooted to the spot, frozen with fear, so was completely helpless as the ferocious animal leapt towards me whilst baring its shiny canines. Its front paws landed on either side of my chest and knocked me to the ground. I was holding my breath so I couldn't scream, but there was a loud thud as my limp body hit the cold, hard floor. Blinking through the pain, I was now face to face with the predator. My hands started to tingle and then what felt like a surge of electricity spread throughout my whole body. I felt dizzy and my vision blurred, but I could still feel the warm breath of the panther on my flushed cheek.

Just when I thought I was going to pass out with fear the overly bright and artificial sports hall lights flickered on and left me temporarily blinded. I blinked furiously, desperate for my vision to come back. And when it did I was greeted by a sea of faces crowding round, all staring at me.

'There was … Did you see … I, uh …' I willed my brain to form a full sentence. My brain felt completely detached from my body. As the room gradually stopped spinning, I noticed some familiar faces. Amber and her friends were sniggering. Matthew looked concerned. The others, (a small group of guys and girls I vaguely recognised from around college) looked mostly shocked. The sea of faces parted and I saw the fierce but beautiful black panther striding towards me again. I felt too faint to stand so tried to shuffle backwards, but my body was too weak. Why was nobody helping me? The panther's steps slowed to a halt and stopped just in front of me. I braced myself in case it pounced again. But then, in the blink of an eye, the beast had vanished and in its place stood Jamie.

'Jamie?' I uttered. Once again I felt like I was going to pass out.

He offered me a hand to help me up off the floor. I was reluctant to take it. Suddenly I didn't feel so trusting of anyone. I got up by myself but Jamie had to catch me when I almost fell again. My body felt strange, almost foreign.

'Does someone want to explain what the hell just happened?' I felt like shouting but my body could only produce a whisper.

Jamie kept his arm around my shoulder as he started to explain. 'Look, I'm so sorry I put you through that Mollie and it's going to take a while to explain, but it's really important that you underst—'

'Oh, for heaven's sake, just show her.' Amber cut him off mid-speech. She shoved her diamante-covered compact mirror in my face. Why was my mum's face staring back at me? What kind of a trick was this? I brought my hands up to my mouth in disbelief and noticed they looked older – like Mum's. Then I ran them through my mum's curly brown hair.

'What has happened to me?'

'Looks like you shifted into your mummy because you were scared,' Amber jeered.

'I WHAT?!'

Jamie stepped in again and put one hand on either shoulder. Well, my mum's shoulders.

'Mollie, look at me. Seriously, look me in the eyes.'

'No, not until someone explains what just happened,' I said whilst desperately trying to shrug him off.

'Mollie, I need you to calm down first so we can change you back.'

'Calm down? CALM DOWN?!' I was finding my voice now.

'Okay, fine. I'll give it to you straight. You're a shapeshifter. We all are. I had my suspicions about you so I invited you here to see whether I was right. Shifting can be brought on by intense emotions, like fear or embarrassment, you see. We can all shift into animals but it would appear that you're, well, special. You can shift between human forms.'

I'm not sure why he was still talking. My thoughts started reeling as soon as he said "shapeshifter".

I think Matthew could see me starting to panic again so he stepped in. 'Mollie, I'll explain everything later. Please just look at me. Good. Now take a deep breath in through your nose and out through your mouth. Good, let's do it together. Just relax.'

Somehow he managed to calm me down. After around five deep breaths I felt more tingling all over my body but it was gentler this time.

'Good, you're back,' Matthew said with a warm smile. Then he was pulled to the side by Jamie and they appeared to be having a disagreement.

I still had no idea what was going on and just stood silently, concentrating on my breathing so I didn't freak out again. Was this all one big joke to Jamie? To impress Amber maybe? One thing was for sure, I wouldn't be going to korfball training again.

Everyone else in the sports hall was whispering and staring at me. I felt so alone. Thankfully Matthew came up behind me, put a friendly hand on my shoulder and guided me out of the hall. We walked out of the college into the brisk evening air. Matthew put his jacket round my shoulders. He needn't have bothered, my body was still numb from shock. We walked along narrow tree lined paths until we ended up in a local children's playground. My heart ached as I remembered all the time I had spent here with Dad. The seesaw was always our favourite. Luckily, right now the playground was deserted. Neither I nor Matthew had said a word since leaving the college.

As we took a seat on some rusty swings I broke the silence. 'Matthew, I think I'm going mad. This evening I thought a black panther pounced on me but then it turned into Jamie, and then I turned into my mum. But that's just crazy, right?'

Matthew looked at me inquisitively. I could tell he didn't know what approach to take with me to keep me calm.

'Yep, that's pretty crazy,' he replied slowly.

I laughed, slightly manically. 'Good, so there must be a perfectly reasonable explanation for everything that happened?'

'Mollie, Jamie was telling the truth. You are a shapeshifter,' Matthew said before pausing to gauge my reaction.

'I don't know what kind of cruel prank this is and why you're lying to me, Matthew. I thought we were friends. But because I like you I'm going to humour you. Go ahead, why don't you tell me more.'

'Okay. There are around a thousand shapeshifters living in England. We don't know how many there are in the world. Shapeshifting has been mentioned in mythology as far back as the sixteenth century. But shapeshifting has remained just that to most of the world – a myth. There is a register of shapeshifters in England and a committee that runs the group. Around five years ago it was decided that shapeshifters should reveal themselves to the English government. We thought that humans were ready to know the truth and would be accepting of us. We just wanted to live in peace and not have to hide our true selves.'

Matthew looked down at the woodchip floor beneath the swing. I could see his eyes were glistening with tears. What if he was telling the truth? This was all undoubtedly utterly crazy, but what reason did he have to lie?

'Anyway,' he continued, 'the meeting with the government did not go well. The committee never revealed exactly what happened but everyone was told to continue to keep their shapeshifting abilities secret. The humans clearly weren't ready to accept shapeshifters. They were probably just scared. Understandably, I suppose.'

'Can we go back a bit please? What exactly do you mean by "shapeshifting abilities"?' My head was spinning.

'Shapeshifters are just like normal people, except ... we can change forms. Usually we take the form of an animal. There are much fewer shapeshifters who can change human form, like you. As you saw, Jamie can shift into a black panther. He had to scare you to see if you were a shapeshifter since shifting can be triggered by being really scared or embarrassed, but with practice you can learn to control it.' He paused. 'I'm sorry, is this too much for you?' I didn't have to answer for Matthew to realise the answer to that was a definite "yes".

Matthew got up from his swing and knelt in front of mine. He took my trembling hands in his and I looked into his blue eyes. And I realised I trusted him. No matter how crazy all of this sounded, he was telling me the truth.

'It's fine,' I said with a sigh. 'I guess it kind of makes sense. Those feelings I felt today before I ... changed ... the tingling feeling in my arms and legs, the dizziness, the blurred vision ... I've felt them before when I've been embarrassed.'

'That's what Jamie noticed, especially the Battle of the Bands night. I thought it was just the vodka, but Jamie was convinced otherwise.'

I shot him a look that told him it was too soon to joke. We sat in silence again, neither of us knowing quite what to say. All I could hear was the soft chirping of crickets. I looked up at the bright moon and twinkling stars and thought about how my whole understanding of the world had changed in just one moment. I had no idea what was real anymore.

'Listen,' Matthew said, standing up, 'there's a lot more you need to know but I think that's enough for tonight. The plan was for me to mentor you, but this evening Jamie changed his mind and is now insisting he does it instead.' Was that slight irritation I sensed in his voice? What right do either of them have anyway? Who says I want or need to be mentored?

But I was too drained and overwhelmed to argue. 'Please can you just walk me home?'

'Of course.'

CHAPTER 6

THE REST OF the week was surprisingly normal in comparison. Rose and I ate lunch together most days and I resisted the temptation to tell her what had happened because I barely understood it myself. Matthew and I continued to get told off for chatting in maths class, although we avoided talking about what happened in the sports hall. Amber continued to sneer at me whenever we passed in the corridor. And Jamie went back to acting as though I was invisible, to the point he walked straight into me in the corridor and sent my books flying to the ground.

'Sorry,' he muttered as he stepped aside and went to carry on walking.

I spun around to face him. 'No, Jamie. Sorry isn't good enough. We need to talk. I feel like I'm going crazy, and then everyone just acts like nothing happened, but it did happen, and I don't know what to think anymore. I can't carry on like this …' I knew I was rambling but I couldn't stop myself. Jamie's friend who he had been walking with just stood and watched, undoubtedly wondering why his friend was entertaining a madwoman.

'Mollie, take a breath.' There was a hint of annoyance in his voice. 'We can't talk here.'

'Then when?' I asked, trying not to sound as desperate as I felt.

'Korfball training tonight. Meet me fifteen minutes early in the sports hall.'

It clearly wasn't up for discussion as he strode away without waiting for my response. His friend looked back at me over his shoulder with a pitying look.

Okay, so that wasn't an ideal interaction but at least I only had half a day to wait until I hopefully got some answers. I was still so confused by it all. How were these transformations physically possible? What was I supposed to do with this new "skill"? If shapeshifters are real, does that mean witches and vampires are real too? I had spent my evenings on Google but naturally it wasn't providing many answers.

The rest of the day dragged as I watched the clock tick down to the end of chemistry. I couldn't concentrate on the experiment and my hair had multiple near misses with the Bunsen burner. When the bell rang I practically ran to the changing room, threw on my sports kit and tied up my hair. This time when I entered the sports hall the lights were on and Jamie was practising his shooting down the far end. He threw me the ball as I got nearer and I took a shot which hit the front of the basket.

'Aim higher,' he said.

I did, and I scored.

'Better,' he said.

We continued to pass the ball between us and take shots as Jamie talked.

'Each team has eight players on the court at any one time. There are two girls and two guys in attack, and two girls and two guys in defence. They swap roles after every two goals scored. Unlike basketball or netball the basket, or "korf" as it is technically called, is a third of the way in from the baseline, so you can shoot from any angle. You can't run with the ball or dribble but there is a move a bit like a basketball layup which is called a runner. Also, if you—'

'Stop,' I uttered, interrupting his monologue. 'Just stop.'

'Sorry, was that too much information?' he asked so calmly, which irritated me even more because he must have known what I actually wanted, in fact desperately needed, to talk about.

'Why are you telling me all this?' I asked.

'Because korfball is our cover-up. And it needs to look convincing to outsiders, so you actually need to be able to play. Training is a safe space where we can talk, bond and work on our special abilities. But sometimes we actually do just play korfball because it's escapism for us, it keeps us fit and helps us let off steam.' Jamie showed off by passing the ball behind his back and between his legs before scoring. 'Plus, you have your first match this weekend,' he added.

Jamie winked and smiled at me for the first time all evening. I wish he would show his softer side more often.

'Listen,' he continued, 'I'm sorry I'm being evasive. It's just that we haven't had a new member in a while, especially not one as … talented as you. It's hard to know where to begin.'

'You don't think this is hard for *me*?' I asked. I just needed some honesty so I could start to process it all.

'Of course,' he finally conceded. 'Come and sit down over here.'

We sat down on a wooden bench on the side of the court. Jamie stared at the korfball as he repetitively turned it over in his hands.

'I know Matthew gave you some information about shapeshifters and why we have to live in secret. My father is on the Shifters committee and was one of the main people who wanted us to reveal ourselves to the world so we could live in peace and without fear. He was so disappointed when the meeting with the government didn't go as planned. Don't get me wrong, being able to shift is a great ability, but it comes with its dangers. Like being caught by a non-shifter who doesn't understand. And then there's the Drifters …'

'The who?' I had decided to suspend all my disbelief for the time being so I could absorb all the information I was finally being given.

'Okay, so most shapeshifters can change form to an

animal, like my animal is a—'

'I'm perfectly aware of what you can shift to,' I said, half-jokingly.

'Oh yeah, sorry about that. My point is, few shapeshifters can change between different human forms like you can. The Drifters, as they're known, think they are above other Shifters as well as humans and are ultimately plotting to take over the country. They have taken themselves off the Shifter's registry and given themselves new identities. Drifters can be anyone they want, any time they want. They use their power for evil and committing crimes like robberies. They can just change identities so they never get caught. So now they are all filthy rich.'

I felt so shocked that all this could be going on in the world and the majority of the population had no idea. I kind of wished I could go back to my state of blissful ignorance.

'Why are the Drifters so awful?' I asked. 'Why wouldn't they use their power for good?'

'They weren't happy when they weren't accepted by the human government and now they think the world owes them a favour. And they think the rest of us Shifters who don't have their abilities are just jealous of them.'

I stared at the floor, trying to process everything. I was concentrating so hard I barely felt Jamie rest his hand on my leg.

'Mollie, this next bit is important. Once the Drifters

find out about you, they are likely to come after you. They have big, elaborate plans to take control of the country so they want all shapeshifters with human shifting abilities on board. Forcefully, if not willingly.'

He emphasised the last sentence and a chill ran down my spine.

'Okay, so what do I do?' I asked.

'Well, firstly, you need to learn to control your ability. I obviously don't have any experience of human shifting but I assume it's similar to animal shifting. So stand up and face me.' I did as I was told. 'Good. Now, you're going to shift into me. It's easiest because you can see me, you don't need to work from your memory. Now, study my face.'

Dark hair, strong eyebrows, sharp cheekbones, soft lips. I wasn't sure how long I was meant to study his face for before it became weird.

'Now, close your eyes and clear your mind,' Jamie continued. 'Focus on each part of your body from your head to your toes and imagine your body changing form.'

How could I clear my mind when I was standing here in front of Jamie with my eyes closed. I felt so vulnerable. *Focus Mollie.* I wanted to get this right and impress Jamie.

I opened my eyes. Jamie was smiling.

'Does that mean it worked?' I asked hopefully.

'It's just like looking in a mirror,' Jamie replied. 'Spin around. I've never seen myself from all angles before!'

I tried to comply but my body felt so foreign. My legs

were heavy and I nearly tripped over my new larger feet as I tried to turn around.

'Woah, okay, take it easy,' Jamie said. 'Let's get you back to normal. Close your eyes again. Deep breath in and as you breathe out relax your muscles.'

I did just as Jamie said. Nothing. My heart rate quickened. Please don't let me be stuck like this. What a disaster. *Relax, Mollie, relax.*

'I can't do it!' I said, as I looked down and realised I was still in Jamie's body.

'Yes you can. You've done the hard part. Now just breathe. Take your time.'

Eventually I felt a tingle run through me from my head to my toes.

I tentatively opened one eye and saw that Jamie was smiling again. 'Perfect,' he said. How did Jamie always stay so calm? I felt completely drained.

There was so much more I wanted to ask but we were interrupted by the rest of the team bounding into the sports hall. First there was Amber, looking immaculate as ever, followed by her friends, Clara and Emma. There was one more girl who had long dark glossy hair and a beautiful smile. She introduced herself as Ava and gave me a friendly hug. There were two guys I vaguely recognised from around college. One was called Ed. He had a head full of dark curly hair and kind eyes. The other guy was called Will; he was tall and slim and seemed very laid back, and he greeted me with a high five.

And then, of course, there was Matthew.

'Welcome to the team!' Matthew beamed. Everyone clapped and cheered, except for Amber.

'Amber, play nice,' Jamie warned, which was met with an eye roll.

Everyone dispersed to do some shooting practice. I felt a bit lost and out of place before Ava pulled me aside for a chat. 'How are you feeling?' she asked.

'Um, that's difficult to describe! I feel like my whole world has been turned upside down. How do I even start to process this?'

'You take your time. And you lean on the team. We've all been through it. Although I found out a few years ago as my mum is a shapeshifter too. It made things a little easier having that support at home I suppose, although it was a lot to process at just thirteen. I remember Mum sat me down and gave me all the usual "growing up" talks and then at the end she was just like, "Oh yeah, and also, you will have the ability to turn into an animal"!'

'Wow!' was all I could respond.

I had so many questions for her, but they would have to wait as Ed called out to the group, 'Should we go for a run outside? Show Mollie what we can do?'

'Sure, that's a good idea,' Jamie replied.

Matthew came and stood by my side. 'I should explain, during these sessions we sometimes practice korfball, but more often we shift and give our animal forms a run about. If we don't shift for a period of time it starts to become uncomfortable, like an itch that needs to be scratched. We shift, then sneak out the back of the sports hall and run together through the fields and woods. Amber keeps watch from above to avoid us coming into contact with humans or other animals.'

Amber must have been eavesdropping as she chimed in, 'And how exactly is Mollie going to keep up?'

'She can ride with me,' Matthew replied simply.

'No, she's better off with me,' Jamie insisted. Matthew and Jamie stared at each other unblinking for an uncomfortable length of time. Eventually Matthew uttered, 'Sure,' through gritted teeth.

Jamie, Matthew and the others arranged themselves in a line in front of me.

'Is everyone ready?' Jamie asked.

And then, it was like I was dreaming. A lot of strange things had happened to me recently but this was still probably most shocking of all. In a matter of seconds there were no longer eight people standing in front of me but eight animals. Where Jamie had stood there was a familiar black panther. In Matthew's place was a grey wolf. Where Amber had stood there was now a majestic owl hovering overhead. In Clara's place was a lynx and in Emma's a deer. In Ava's place stood a towering horse with a long black mane. In Will's place was a greyhound. And finally, at the end of the line there stood a warthog. Although I was in shock I found myself thinking that poor Ed had drawn the short straw.

It really was the most surreal sight. Panther Jamie took a few paces towards me and I could hear him panting. My body was tingling all over and I felt rooted to the spot with fear, again. Wolf Matthew then came right up to me and looked up into my eyes. We held eye contact until I began to feel calmer. I could tell that it was Matthew in there behind those beautiful blue eyes. Instinctively, I lifted my hand and placed it on the back of his neck. The fur was thick and smooth.

Panther Jamie broke me from my trance by giving me a nudge with his hind legs. He seemed to be encouraging me to climb on his back. Against all my better judgements I did so. I sat gently in the middle of his back but as soon as he began to move I lay forwards and wrapped my arms around his neck. Panther Jamie, with me on his back, headed out of the rear door of the sports hall and the other animals followed. We then made our way quickly and quietly across the college playing fields to the shelter of the woodlands. It was a dark evening with only a glint of light coming from the almost full moon and I could barely see, but I assumed most of the animals had better night vision than me.

Whoooosh! All of a sudden panther Jamie started sprinting and I was holding on round his neck for dear life. All I could hear was the wind rushing past my ears and occasionally the panting of the other animals. Incredibly, Ed and his short warthog legs were keeping up. After a while I actually started to enjoy myself. The whole situation was ludicrous and terrifying and yet, as I felt the wind in my hair, I also felt free and invincible. I couldn't even imagine how many miles we must have covered before all the animals came to a stop in a clearing in the woods and then shifted back to their human forms.

'Five minute break,' Jamie said. 'Catch your breath.'

I stumbled over to Matthew. My legs felt like jelly. 'This is so bizarre,' I admitted. 'Amazing, but bizarre. Riding through the woods on a black panther. Not something I ever thought I would do, but totally amazing.' I think the adrenaline rush was making me ramble.

'You should have ridden with me,' Matthew said sulkily. 'I can actually run faster than Jamie you know.'

'I didn't realise it was a race. What's really going on, Matthew?'

Matthew leaned in towards me and lowered his voice to ensure no one would overhear. 'I just think it's strange,' Matthew began, 'that Jamie showed very little interest in you until he discovered you can change human forms. I'm sure he would have let me mentor you if you had been an animal shifter like the rest of us.'

'Thanks for looking out for me. You're a good friend, but everything's fine, really.' My heart raced when Matthew implied that Jamie was interested in me.

As if on cue, Jamie came striding over, his forehead glistening with sweat. 'You managing to keep up alright,

Matthew?' Jamie teased, as Matthew scowled in response.

'Condescending little …' I heard Matthew mutter under his breath.

Jamie seemingly hadn't heard. He took me by the hand and led me away. 'Come on, we're going to head back now.'

It felt like we were travelling even faster on the way back. The cold air hit me in the face and my eyes started to water. However, I was still a little disappointed when the experience came to an end. All the animals snuck back into the sports hall after owl Amber had given the go ahead from above. Once everyone was back in the safety of the sports hall, they started to shift back to their human forms. I noticed most of them were still trying to catch their breath. I was so fascinated by the transformations of the others that I forgot where I was. In a split second, I dropped half a metre and found myself lying on the floor with my arms wrapped around human Jamie's neck. He just looked at me, bemused, until I unfroze and scrambled off him.

'Good work tonight. Everyone okay?' Jamie asked. Everyone nodded. Except me. I couldn't exactly say I was "okay" just yet. Jamie signalled for everyone to leave so we were alone again. Amber looked mildly irritated by this as she sauntered out of the door. Jamie was still standing quite close to me; I hadn't moved away, but neither had he. I waited for him to say something but instead he leaned in and kissed me. His lips were as soft as they looked. I was caught off guard and felt a familiar tingling in my fingertips. *Do not shift now, Mollie. Whatever you do, not now.* His kiss slowed a little and I was able to regain my composure. Eventually, Jamie pulled away. 'That was great,' he said quite matter-of-factly.

'Oh, well, I, uh, thanks,' I mumbled.

'You're getting the hang of controlling your shifting already, even under intense emotional stress,' Jamie continued.

Now I was highly confused. Does he like me or was that purely a test? I think he likes me. I think.

Jamie strode off towards the door whilst saying, 'We've got a match on Sunday, come along and sit on the bench.' Before I could respond, he was gone.

The sports hall suddenly felt overwhelmingly empty and silent so I hurried out after Jamie. He was stood by the car drop-off point at the front of the college, talking with another man. It was dark but from what I could make out the man looked like an older version of Jamie.

Initially I couldn't hear their conversation but then Jamie's dad started to raise his voice. 'You took her out on your run? You're supposed to be teaching her to control her ability and preparing her for the Drifters. She's not like the rest of you, Jamie. She's special.'

'Thanks a lot, Dad,' Jamie grumbled.

'I'm sorry, son. You know what I mean.'

I really didn't want to get involved but I needed to

walk by them to get home. I put my hood up and tried to sneak past.

'Mollie?' Jamie's dad called out. Apparently I wasn't sneaky enough. My stomach flipped. How did he even recognise me?

'Oh, hello, Mr Peterson,' I said, as I pulled my hood back down and tried to compose myself.

'Please, call me Paul. Jamie has told me all about you.'

I blushed. 'Oh, really?'

'Whilst I have every faith that my son will guide you through these tough times, you are in a very unique situation, and so if you ever need anything, anything at all, please do come straight to me.'

'Dad, stop interfering. I can do it,' Jamie said, looking uncharacteristically uncomfortable.

'Jamie has been very kind to me so far, but thank you for your offer,' I said politely. I was struggling to work out the dynamic between Jamie and his dad and I didn't want to say anything to make the situation any more awkward.

'Let me know what Jamie has taught you,' Jamie's dad said, 'and I can fill in the gaps. Knowledge is power after all.'

'Oh, well, I, uh.' I felt completely on the spot and didn't know what to say. Jamie's dad had Jamie's intense stare, but it was even more intimidating somehow.

'Umm, can I just have a quick chat with Mollie, Dad? Alone?' Jamie asked.

'Of course, son. I'll wait in the car. It was a pleasure

meeting you, Mollie,' Jamie's dad said whilst giving me a firm handshake.

'I'm sorry,' Jamie whispered to me, 'Dad is a little … controlling … He's used to being in charge and looking after people and he struggles to let go. He means well. I just wish he had a bit more faith in me.'

'I have faith in you,' I replied, looking up into his eyes and Jamie held my gaze, unblinking until his dad started up the engine in a not-so-subtle signal for Jamie to get in the car.

'I would offer you a lift,' Jamie said, 'but I wouldn't want to put you through more interrogation.'

'It's fine, really. I could use the fresh air. I'll see you on Sunday.'

I walked home in a bit of a trance, a million thoughts running through my mind. I wished I could talk to Rose about it all. She always knows the right thing to say.

When I got home I slipped my trainers off silently by the front door and tried to sneak straight up the stairs to my room. Somehow Mum caught me. 'Good evening, my love. How was korfball training?' she asked.

'Fine, thanks. Good. Tiring. I was going to get an early night, if that's okay?'

'Of course, but come and say a quick hello to the book club ladies first, will you?'

'Do I have to?' I mouthed silently.

Mum just raised her eyebrows in a way which said, "Stop being a rude, petulant child".

I put on a big fake smile as I opened the living room door. 'Good evening, everyone,' I beamed at the five women who all smiled back. Considering this was meant to be a book club, there seemed to be a distinct lack of books and a clear abundance of wine glasses. I vaguely recognised the women, but Mum doesn't like to host book club too often as she feels inadequate and says that everyone else has much nicer, bigger houses than us. I've told her not to be silly and that she should have people round, so was pleased she had seemed to listen to my advice.

'Mollie has just been at korfball training,' Mum told the other women proudly.

'Oh what's that?' one of them asked.

'It's a bit of a mixture of netball and basketball,' I said, hoping that was a satisfactory enough explanation.

'Oh, that sounds interesting.'

'It is definitely interesting.'

'And it keeps you out of trouble I suppose! Your mum told us you got a little carried away at a college event recently …'

I knew the comment wasn't meant maliciously but I was mortified that mum was telling these women about my embarrassing life. Plus, it was a bit rich of them to judge my drinking given the number of empty wine bottles littering the room.

'You must be tired, Mollie,' Mum said, likely feeling guilty for talking about me and so offering me an escape.

'Why don't you go and get ready for bed?'

'Good night, Mollie. Sweet dreams!' the tipsy women all called out as I climbed the stairs.

My dreams weren't exactly sweet. I dreamt I was running through a forest, being chased by a pack of animals and no matter how hard I tried, I couldn't find a way out and I kept tripping on tree roots. I suppose you don't need to be a psychologist to work that one out.

CHAPTER 7

SUNDAY SOON ROLLED around and at midday I Ieft my house and made my way to my first korfball match. The early Autumn air was cool and I quickly realised that I should have worn a coat. My muddy trainers crunched on the colourful leaves underfoot and I quickened my pace, not wanting to be late. When I entered the sports hall the court was set up for a match with a post at either end and players from both teams were starting to warm up. We were playing against a local college, the Hammerford Hawks. Their kit was blue and ours, the Tanglewood Tigers, was red. The Hawks looked like a strong team and most of their shots were floating straight through the basket.

I walked up to Matthew who was tying the laces of his fancy trainers at the side of the court. 'Sorry to have to tell you this,' I began, 'but they look really good. Are you nervous?'

Matthew looked up at me and grinned. 'Nah,' he replied. 'We have certain "skills" which have ensured we have been unbeaten over the past two years.' He must have noticed my quizzical look and quietly continued, 'Shifters can be very speedy and agile. We just need to know how to channel those traits of our animals without shifting completely. Of course we need to make it look natural, but if we ever find ourselves a couple of goals down, we can rely on these skills to get us back in the game.'

'Well, I look forward to observing your incredible speed and agility from the bench,' I said.

I joined the rest of the team for the warm up. Unfortunately, my shooting was not on form and I didn't feel very speedy or agile. Ava probably looked the most naturally sporty of all the Shifters and she darted around the court with ease. Poor Ed looked like he was struggling to keep up at times although he didn't stop trying and smiling.

Five minutes before the game, Jamie called everyone together for a team talk. We huddled together in a circle. I ended up next to Jamie and he put one of his muscular arms around my shoulders. On his other side he put his other arm around Amber. Next to her was Clara, then Emma, then Ava, then Ed and finally Matthew. Wait, someone's missing.

'Where's Will?' Jamie asked.

Everyone looked at each other blankly, clearly none the wiser. There were only five minutes left until the game was due to start.

'Great,' Jamie said sarcastically, 'we're a boy short.

What are we going to do?'

More blank looks until it seemed as though the Shifters all had the exact same thought at the same time as they all turned their heads and looked at me.

Eventually the penny dropped. 'You want me to shift into Will, don't you? No, uh no, no way,' I garbled.

Jamie pulled me round to face him. 'I know you can do this. You're ready.'

'I really don't think I am,' I replied. 'And there are people watching. What if I mess the shifting up?'

There were viewing stands around the court and although there weren't many people watching there were enough to make me feel nervous. Even Rose was sitting in the front row, there especially to cheer me on.

Matthew took me away from the circle and I was grateful to have some space to think. 'You don't have to do this,' he said. 'No pressure. But it would be good practice for you to hone your shifting skills. Go to the changing rooms and visualise Will. Go over every physical detail from his head to his toes and try to feel your body changing at the same time. You want the transformation to be quick but controlled.'

'No pressure you say?' I joked as I glanced back over to see the rest of the team all looking at me hopefully. 'Fine, I'll try.'

I jogged nervously out of the hall back into the girls' changing room and sat down on the cold, hard changing bench. I closed my eyes and visualised Will. Scruffy dark-brown hair, brown eyes, toned arms, long legs. Nothing was happening. Typical. I screwed my eyes up as tight as I could and concentrated on willing my body to change form. Suddenly a familiar tingle ran through my body. I opened my eyes and dashed over to the mirror. Yes! I did it! I felt an odd mixture of pride, excitement, fear and horror. It really is the strangest thing to look in the mirror and see an entirely different person staring back at you.

A girl from the Hammerford Hawks entered the changing room and let out a little shriek when she saw me. Oh no, had I not shifted right? I looked down. I had shorts on at least. After a couple of seconds I caught on to the issue.

'I'm so sorry,' I said, my new deep voice surprising me. 'I was just, uh, leaving …' I put my head down and scuttled out of the girls' changing room.

My new longer limbs felt alien to me and it took all my concentration to get them under control. When I re-entered the sports hall the teams were lining up ready to start. Jamie jogged over to me and whispered, 'Mollie, is that you?' I nodded. He looked me up and down and smiled. 'Good work, now let's see how you can play.'

Korfball teams are split into two divisions and I was with Jamie, Amber and Clara. We started in attack. The referee blew his whistle and Jamie passed the ball to Clara on his left, who in turn passed to Amber. I made a quick, sharp movement to make space to receive the ball from

Amber. Well, as quick and sharp as I could with my new legs which I felt a bit wobbly on. Amber threw the ball hard and fast and just far enough away that I really had to reach for it.

'Agh,' I involuntarily grunted as the ball slipped straight through my fingers and off the side of the court. Amber shrugged her shoulders at me and mouthed, 'Sorry,' but it didn't seem like a genuine apology to me.

The Hammerford Hawks passed the ball to the other end of the court where Matthew, Ed, Ava and Emma now had to defend. Matthew seemed very confident, staying close to his opponent at all times and communicating well with the rest of his division. It made me want to be better. I just needed to feel more connected and in tune with my new body. Matthew successfully intercepted the ball. Amber ran up towards the halfway line gesturing for the ball, but Matthew ignored her and looked at me instead, signalling to me with his eyes to run towards him. As I did so he passed the ball and I caught it! That was the start of a good attack for us which resulted in an impressive goal from Jamie. The opposition soon got a goal back; a long shot against Ed which he couldn't have done much about.

After every two goals the attack and defence swap ends of the court and roles so I found myself in defence. The guy I was marking was shorter than me but he was fast and I had to concentrate hard to coordinate my limbs and keep up with him without tripping over. I tried my best but I ended up conceding a goal. Amber gave me a scornful look. Jamie didn't seem too annoyed; he walked over and gave me a pat on the back. Amber can keep her opinions to herself. I'd like to see her do any better under such circumstances. The game continued to be close, with the goals alternating between teams and the scores were level at half time.

We huddled together for a half-time talk. The huddle was much sweatier than it had been pre-match. Proof that everyone was working hard, I suppose. Jamie didn't give a tactical team talk, instead he just said, 'You all know what to do. Time to channel your skills.' I noticed Ed smiling and apparently so did Jamie as he said, 'Keep it subtle Ed. Don't go overboard like last time. We don't want to raise suspicions.'

Ava must have seen my bemused expression and whispered to me, 'Last match Ed really turned up his speed and agility in the second half and scored eleven goals. Not so subtle! You just keep doing what you're doing; you're doing great.'

I didn't believe Ava that I was doing "great" exactly, but I had been generally keeping up with the team and I hoped I was doing Will proud in his absence. It was harder, however, to keep up in the second half as the Shifters channelled the speed and agility of their animals. They were running past their players with ease, much to the annoyance of the Hawks. I could tell the others were really enjoying themselves and I understood why the sport was so important to them for letting off steam and bonding, as well as a cover up for their meetings. I started to enjoy myself too and even scored a goal; I managed to grab a rebound from a missed shot and popped it in the basket, thanks to my new-found height advantage.

The game finished 22–14 in our favour. I could tell the Hawks were confused as to how things went so downhill for them in the second half. I felt a bit sorry for them; it was hardly a level playing field and they had absolutely no idea. We shook hands with them and then high-fived each other as we bundled out of the sports hall.

I had wanted to go over and say hello to Rose but remembered I needed to shift back first. I followed the guys into their changing room, hoping to find a quiet corner where I could shift back. I popped my head behind a row of lockers but I couldn't do it there, it was still too exposed. I walked back round to the main changing area and woah! Talk about too exposed! The guys from both teams were all stripping off and wrapping towels around their waists to head to the shower. There was so much body hair and testosterone, I didn't know where to look. I averted my eyes and tried to push my way to the door. I accidentally bumped into someone. I looked up to apologise and realised it was Jamie. Wearing nothing but a towel. I was mortified, but he seemed completely unbothered. Had he forgotten it was me inside Will's body or was he so confident in his body that he just didn't care?

I pushed on through out of the boys' changing room and then out round the back of the sports hall. The fresh air was a great relief. I took a deep breath in and relaxed for the first time since the start of the match. I scanned the area to make sure it was clear. I continued to take deep breaths as I relaxed each muscle in my body in turn and concentrated on returning to myself. After a few seconds I opened my eyes and looked down at my hands. It seemed to have worked. I felt a lot more comfortable.

Once I had caught my breath, I walked round to the front of the college to meet with the others.

'Hey, Mollie. Nice to have you back,' Matthew called out.

'It's nice to be back,' I replied.

Then Jamie came over and put his arm around me. His hair was still wet from the shower and it made him look even more attractive, if that was possible. 'Great work today,' he said. 'Thanks for stepping up.' I had a flashback to our run-in in the changing room and felt too flustered to reply. Jamie didn't seem to notice and continued to address the whole group, 'Let's go have our meeting somewhere more private and celebrate another win.'

For some unknown reason (maybe I was still high on adrenaline), I offered for everyone to come to my house. I really hoped Mum was still out at her yoga class as usual.

Just as we were setting off back to my house, Will

came striding over with his sports bag slung over his shoulder and said, 'Hey gang. Is everyone ready for the big game?' Cue a lot of blank expressions from the rest of the group until realisation dawned and he said, 'I got the wrong time, didn't I? Not again!'

Everyone laughed as Will threw his arms in the air in disbelief.

'Don't worry,' Jamie said. 'We found an excellent substitute for you. If anyone else asks, you definitely did play in the match. You even scored a goal!'

'Huh?' Will said, understandably confused.

Ed put an arm round Will's shoulder and said, 'Come back to Mollie's house and we'll explain everything.'

Matthew walked home beside me. 'Do you want me to carry your bag?' he asked.

'I'm fine, thank you though. Well played today. You're all so good I could barely keep up, especially in the second half!'

'No way. You were amazing; to play your first match whilst shifted must have been so tough.'

Matthew was right. I should allow myself to feel a little bit proud.

'So, how exactly do you "channel your inner animal" but avoid shifting completely?' I asked, genuinely fascinated by the ability.

'It's really hard to explain,' Matthew said, 'but it takes up so much more energy to do that rather than fully shift as you're constantly trying to maintain the right balance between your human and animal forms.'

'And when you are fully shifted, what's it like? Can you still think like a human or are you thinking in "wolf speak"?'

Matthew laughed. 'No, my thoughts remain the same, it's just my body that changes.'

'What about your family? Are they shapeshifters too?' I asked. I hoped Matthew didn't mind my interrogation, but it was all so new and incredible to me.

'My dad is a shapeshifter, but my mum and little sister aren't. We've kept it hidden from them. Dad's never wanted to burden them and he wants them to have a normal life.'

'That must be tough,' I said.

I wanted to find out more but we had arrived at my house so I pushed open the front door and rushed inside to have a quick tidy up. I had to apologise to the others that me and Mum didn't do a lot of entertaining so all I could offer them was squash and some plain biscuits I found at the back of a cupboard. I put the biscuits on a plate so no one could see from the packet that they were also slightly out of date.

As I was making drinks I felt my phone buzz in my jeans pocket. It was a message from Rose;

Hi stranger. I went to the match today especially to see you, what happened, is everything ok? xx

I felt bad. I hadn't spent nearly as much time with

Rose as I used to since my world had been turned upside down. And it's not like I could tell her what was happening. It's not that I didn't trust her but I wouldn't know where to start. I made a mental note to text her back later.

The rest of the team seemed happy enough and settled themselves in the living room, scattered between the sofa and the floor. They boys were still winding Will up about missing the match, which he took in good humour.

'I would like to nominate Mollie for MVP!' Ed declared.

'Seconded!' said Ava.

'Thanks,' I said. 'I suppose I should dedicate it to Will; I couldn't have done it without him!'

Jamie broke through the laughter as he said, 'Time for business.' The room quietened immediately and everyone looked at him expectantly. 'Firstly, did everyone see the news story yesterday about the jewellery store robbery?'

'The one where the corrupt manager just walked out with a million pounds worth of jewellery?' Amber asked.

'Yes,' Jamie said. 'And don't you think that's odd? That the jewellery shop manager would just rob the store in broad daylight and not even try to cover his tracks?'

'Drifters!' everyone whispered.

'Exactly,' Jamie said. 'That poor shop keeper is looking at up to five years in prison. He has an alibi, his wife insists he was at home with her all day, but since his face was captured clearly on the store CCTV, the police don't believe her. She will probably end up getting jail time too.'

'That's so sad,' Ava said. 'I read that they have children too.'

'And all so the Drifters can line their own dirty pockets,' Matthew said, shaking his head.

'Fortunately, there is also some good news,' Jamie said. 'As most of you know, my dad and the rest of the Shifter's committee have been working on an anti-shifting serum that, when ingested by a Drifter, will change them back to their original form, only older and frailer as they have been shifted out of their original form for so long.'

He said that like it was the most normal thing in the world.

Jamie continued. 'They've been working on it for years, but they finally think they're close to perfecting the formula. They've struggled to make it potent enough to disarm the Drifters and strip them of their powers whilst not killing them, as that's not their aim.'

Just as I was processing all that, Jamie turned to me and said, 'Dad has also been worrying about you. He wants us all to be extra vigilant to any Drifters that might be snooping around. Once news gets round of your abilities the Drifters will try to track you down.'

'I'll just stop shifting then. I never asked for this "special ability" you know,' I said, a bit moodily.

'No,' Jamie said, 'As much as shifting could get you

into trouble, it can also get you out of trouble if you learn how to control it properly. And it could be used to do so much good.'

I nodded to indicate I understood. What I didn't understand was how I ended up being so different when all I ever wanted was to fit in. I didn't want to seem ungrateful, but I would gladly have given up my "gift" to anyone who wanted it. Trying to fit in at college was proving hard enough without having to worry about the threat of a group of evil shapeshifters.

Jamie must have sensed my mood. 'Mollie, are you okay? Can we go somewhere private for a chat?'

'Uh, okay. Let's go upstairs,' I said.

I was too worn out from the match to worry about the state of my bedroom. I opened the door and Jamie stepped inside. Suddenly, I felt a little nervous and wished my room was a bit more stylish and grown up. Jamie started to pace around my room looking at the photos I had stuck to my walls with Blu Tack (much to Mum's annoyance). Most were of me and Rose, but one photo in particular had caught his eye – the one of Dad holding me as a baby.

'You've never talked about your dad,' Jamie said, still staring at the wall.

'That's because he left us with no explanation when I was eleven and I haven't seen him since,' I replied matter-of-factly.

'Wow, that must have been hard,' Jamie said whilst

turning to look at me with genuine concern. It was nice to see a softer side to him but it took me by surprise and I turned away, blushing.

'So how come I was so late to find out I'm a shapeshifter?' I asked.

'Well sometimes it runs in families, like mine, so my dad told me when I was thirteen. It was a tough time but at least I had Dad to guide me.'

'What is your dad's animal?' I asked. I had been imagining him as some kind of big cat like Jamie, but I realised I actually had no idea.

'He's an eagle,' Jamie said, rather sullenly.

'Wow, that's so cool, no?'

'Yeah, it is, but Dad was really disappointed when I turned out to be a land animal and not able to fly like him. He tried to hide it but the disappointment was written over his face for years,' Jamie said, looking genuinely pained by the memories. 'But anyway, this isn't about me. As I was saying, sometimes shapeshifting runs in families, but sometimes it's just a random genetic abnormality.' Jamie paused. 'I mean that in the nicest possible way. You should talk with Amber. She only found out a year ago and it was a shock to her too. None of her family are shapeshifters either.'

I think the look on my face gave away how I felt about the idea of having a heart to heart with Amber.

Jamie came and sat down next to me on my bed and rested his hand on my knee. 'Mollie, you have been so strong over the past couple of weeks and the way you've handled all the changes in your life is pretty incredible. And just so you know, I don't give out compliments very often.'

'I'd noticed!'

He smiled at me, a genuine smile that reached his eyes, and this time he was the one who seemed a little embarrassed. 'I want you to know I will always try to protect you. You can trust me.' He looked into my eyes again and I believed him.

Just as I thought he might lean in and kiss me again there was a knock at my door.

'Molliiie,' Amber's voice called through. 'I'm so sorry to interrupt, but would you mind coming back down-stairs, we've run out of squash.'

Somehow, I suspected she wasn't sorry at all. I looked at Jamie apologetically, then stomped downstairs. Jamie followed me and joined the others in the living room, whilst I went to the kitchen. I searched through the cupboards for a jug but could only find a vase. That would do. I filled it to the brim with squash before passing it to Amber.

'Here you go,' I said with a smile. That should keep her going. Out of the corner of my eye, I caught Jamie smirking.

'Jamie,' Ed said tentatively. 'I've seen a few social media posts recently about "big cat sightings" in the area … you wouldn't know anything about that would you?'

The whole room turned to look at Jamie. He stood up from the sofa arm he was perched on and shuffled uncomfortably. 'Well … I … uh.'

'I thought the rule was that we only shift when we're together. In a controlled environment?' Matthew said frostily.

'It was only a couple of times,' Jamie said. 'I really needed to let off some steam.'

'It risks everyone's cover, though, Jamie. You know that, mate,' Will joined in.

'I know. I apologise. Now, end of discussion, let's talk about something else,' Jamie said, sitting down on the arm of the sofa again.

I saw Matthew get up and storm to the kitchen. I followed him.

'Are you okay?' I asked Matthew, who was leaning against the kitchen counter. He stared out of the window into our unkempt garden.

'It's just annoying. It's always one rule for us, and another rule for him.'

'Maybe he's been having a tough time?' I suggested gently.

'He likes to think he's the leader, so he should be leading by example,' Matthew said, clearly unwilling to consider the situation from another perspective. A couple of seconds later, Matthew shook his head and turned to face me. 'I'm sorry,' he said. 'I'm not usually like this. It's just … me and Jamie are very different people. Being a shapeshifter shoves people together that wouldn't usually have anything to do with each other. It's not always easy.'

'I understand, completely,' I said.

'But,' Matthew continued, 'we mostly make it work. We're like a big dysfunctional family. We have our disagreements, but we're bonded together by something so extraordinary. We'll always be there for each other when needed.'

'And I'm always here for you if you ever need to vent,' I said.

'Thanks Mollie,' Matthew said as we made our way back to join the others in the living room. 'I'm so glad you're one of us.'

CHAPTER 8

M ONDAY MORNING CAME round all too quickly. Luckily, my morning biology class was quite easy and I found myself daydreaming about the events of the weekend rather than concentrating on the life cycle of plants. I bumped into Rose in the corridor after the class (and I mean I literally bumped into her, thanks to my continued day dreaming).

'Oh, hi,' Rose said, her greeting feeling slightly more frosty than usual.

'Uh, I've just remembered, I'm so sorry I didn't reply to your text.'

'That's fine,' Rose said in a tone that suggested it definitely wasn't fine. 'I expected you to have been busy with your new korfball friends anyway.'

'I am genuinely sorry Rose, I've just had a lot going on.'

'So have I, Mollie, and I would really have liked the chance to talk to my best friend about it.'

Rose looked as though she was on the verge of tears and I didn't know what to say to make it better. I moved towards her to give her a hug, but she backed away and scuttled off down the corridor. I wished so much that I could be honest with her, but I wouldn't want to put her in danger. I promised myself I would make it up to her soon.

I had a break before my next class and without Rose to talk to I felt a bit lost. I wandered out the front of the college and thought about going for a short walk up the road to clear my head. But then I heard someone shout my name.

'Mollie! Hey, come and sit with us!' It was Will and he was sat on a bench with Ed. I walked over and squeezed on to the bench next to them.

'We were just talking about you,' Ed admitted.

'Oh, really? What have I done?' I asked.

'Nothing!' Will replied, 'We were just saying how cool it must be,' he looked around and lowered his voice, 'to be able to shift into anyone you want at any time.'

'So cool,' Ed agreed. 'The possibilities are endless.'

'I guess I haven't really had much time to think about it,' I said. 'It's all been a bit of a whirlwind.'

'Yeah, of course. That's understandable,' Ed said.

I was intrigued now. 'So, what *would* you do if you had my ability?'

'Hmm,' Will pondered. 'I would shift into someone super famous and just walk up and down the street, waving at all my adoring fans!'

I had to admit, that did sound fun.

'I'm thinking slightly closer to home,' Ed said. 'Imagine shifting into Principal Golding. Imagine the power!'

'Ooh,' Will said, his eyes lighting up. 'You could give everyone top grades, you could close the college early, you could order pizza for the whole college …'

'Mmm pizza,' Ed said.

They both turned and looked at me.

'You up for some fun?' Will asked. 'If you shift into Mr Golding you could get the receptionist to order a load of pizzas.'

'What would Jamie say, though?' I asked.

'It's fine, just harmless fun, and a chance to practice your shifting,' Ed said.

I wasn't sure, but on the other hand what good was having this special ability if I couldn't have a little fun with it?

'I'm in,' I said, 'but you two will have to distract Mr Golding whilst I talk to the receptionist. I can't risk him bumping into himself.'

'You can count on us,' Will said, holding out his fist for a fist bump.

We made our way back towards the front entrance of the college. I stopped to hide behind a bush to shift whilst Will and Ed kept watch. I imagined Mr Golding's wispy brown, greying hair and his bushy eyebrows. I closed my eyes and concentrated. A familiar tingle ran through me then I opened my eyes and looked down at my grey suit trousers and black leather shoes.

'Hello, Mr Golding,' Will and Ed said laughing as I stepped out from behind the bush.

'Hide back behind the bush,' Ed said, 'whilst we distract him.'

'Okay.' My heart was pounding. I hoped this didn't backfire.

A couple of minutes later I saw Ed, Will and Mr Golding rushing out of the front door and Will saying, 'Over here, Mr Golding. This is where the students were doing drugs …'

I sidled into the college and strode over to the receptionist. I hadn't spoken to her much before. She was middle aged with curly brown hair and wore bright red glasses.

'Hello,' I said, trying to read her name badge, 'Miss Jenkins.'

'Please, Robert, call me Lucy! You haven't come to see me in a while. How have you been?'

Was she flirting with me?

'Oh yes, I'm fine thank you, just busy. You know, with the students.'

'Well, do you want to go out for a drink sometime?'

Wow, I wasn't expecting the conversation to go this way.

'Uh, I think I'm married,' I said looking down at my ring finger on my left hand. 'Yes, I'm married.'

'Well, that didn't stop you last time,' Miss Jenkins said with a wink.

Eurgh, I felt sick.

'I actually just came here to ask you to do something for me please,' I said trying to retain my composure. 'I need you to order pizza for the whole college.'

'Really? Why?'

'Um, because it's National Pizza Day.' I cringed internally. Surely she wasn't going to buy that?

'Oh, okay. How many? Thirty?'

'Make it fifty.'

'Okay, if you're sure.'

'Of course I'm sure.'

'Okay, I will order them now. And let me know about those drinks!' she called out as I hurriedly walked away.

I hid and shifted back just before Mr Golding came back into view, followed by Ed and Will.

'Sorry, Sir,' Will was saying. 'They must have run off.'

Mr Golding looked mildly irritated as he marched back to his office.

'All done?' Ed asked me.

'All done,' I confirmed as we all high-fived.

'See, I knew it would be fun,' Will said.

'Hmm, not entirely fun,' I said. 'I got a little more information than I wanted … Mr Golding and the receptionist are totally doing it.'

'Eurgh, gross,' Will and Ed replied in unison.

We waited in the reception area for the pizzas to arrive and tried not to look too guilty. Amazingly, it only took the pizza place twenty minutes to make and deliver fifty pizzas. The delivery driver staggered up to the college carrying a towering pile of pizza boxes. And that was only half of them.

'Alright love,' he said to the receptionist. 'Where do you want these?'

'We'll take them!' the three of us offered.

As we were gathering up the pizza boxes to take them to the canteen, Mr Golding came out of his office to see what the commotion was.

'What's going on here?' he asked Miss Jenkins.

'It's the pizzas you asked me to order,' she replied.

'I did nothing of the sort! Why would I ask you to order so many pizzas?'

'Er, because it's National Pizza Day?'

'Are you trying to be funny? Who's going to pay for all this?' Mr Golding's face had turned bright red and he was throwing his arms in the air as he spoke. Miss Jenkins just sat behind her desk in a stunned and confused silence.

We snuck away with the pizzas and scurried to the canteen as fast as we could.

'That was awesome!' Ed said.

'So funny,' Will agreed. 'But maybe let's not tell Jamie what we did.'

'Why?' I asked, feeling panicked. 'You said Jamie wouldn't mind.'

'Yeeah,' Ed said. 'We weren't entirely truthful. He would definitely be super annoyed that we pulled a prank.'

I rolled my eyes. 'I should have known you two would get me into trouble! Looks like we need to eat the evidence quickly then!'

I wolfed down as much pizza as I could manage before my maths class, to the point I felt a bit sick. Then I waved goodbye to Will and Ed. I couldn't help but develop soft spots for them both, despite their bad influences.

As I made my way to the maths huts, I passed Mr Golding in the corridor. He was still waving his arms in the air in irritation and confusion.

Luckily, I made it to maths before Miss Hawkins. Matthew greeted me with a beaming smile as I took my seat next to him.

'Have you recovered from the weekend yet?' he asked.

'Physically – just about. Mentally – I'm not sure I will ever recover!'

'That's fair enough,' Matthew said with a grin.

'Do you ever wish you could just be normal?' I asked with a sigh.

'Nah normal's boring. And what is normal anyway?'

'That's true.'

'If you ever need a distraction from all the craziness,' Matthew said, 'I volunteer at an animal rescue centre on Saturdays. We could always do with an extra pair of hands.'

Just when I thought Matthew couldn't be any more

lovely.

'That sounds good,' I replied. 'What animals do you work with?'

'Mostly cats and a few dogs.'

'I thought you hated cats?' I laughed.

'I lied – I love cats! They can be aloof to begin with but once you've gained their trust you have a friend for life.'

'Well, I would love to join you one weekend. Thank you for asking me.'

Matthew's expression turned uncharacteristically serious as he gently placed his hand on top of mine. 'Don't ever feel like you are alone in this. I'm always here, whatever you need.'

I blinked furiously to fight back the tears. Matthew was so kind and so understanding and such a good friend.

'I really—' I started to reply but Miss Hawkins walked in and cut me off.

'Silence now. These equations aren't going to solve themselves! Unless you would like another one of my wonderful maths jokes?'

The whole class groaned in unison.

'Oh, come on,' Miss Hawkins said. 'Not all maths puns are bad … just sum!'

The whole class groaned again and we silently worked on our equations in the hopes we wouldn't be subjected to any more awful jokes.

When lunch time arrived and I walked back into the canteen, I could see Rose sat on her own on the end of a long table. She looked up, gave me a half smile and nodded for me to sit with her. I was so glad she seemed less annoyed and ready to talk.

As I made my way over to sit with Rose, Jamie suddenly appeared in front of me. 'Mollie! I've been looking for you all morning.' This was new. Jamie usually barely acknowledged me in public at college, let alone talked to me in a busy canteen. 'I think we need to spend more time together. I need to tell you everything I know about the Drifters so you're prepared if you encounter one. And we need to work on controlling your shifting.' He paused, then mumbled, 'And, well, I guess I just generally want to get to know you better.'

For once, Jamie didn't seem his usual confident self; he actually seemed a little nervous. I could barely believe it; I made Jamie nervous! A big smile began to spread across my face and there was nothing I could do to stop it.

'So that's a yes, then?' Jamie asked, before clarifying, 'To spending more time together?'

'Sure,' I said with a shrug of my shoulders whilst trying to sound casual. At least he couldn't see how hard my heart was thumping in my chest.

Jamie seemed to snap back to his usual assured self. 'Great, let's start with lunch.' He ushered for me to sit down at the nearest table with him. I had to make a quick judgement call. I knew I had planned to sit with Rose and make amends but there was not one girl in the whole college who would turn down having lunch with Jamie. Rose would understand that, surely? As I sat down opposite Jamie, the look on her face suggested that no, she did not understand, not at all.

'I've heard there's free pizza around. Did you want some?' Jamie asked.

'Oh, actually I'm not all that hungry,' I replied sheepishly.

'Okay, so,' Jamie said quietly, leaning towards me over the table, 'let me tell you a bit about the Drifters. Most of them are pretty old but they spend the majority of their time shifted as stunningly beautiful younger men and women. Be vigilant, it's very likely they already know about you; news travels fast in our small community.'

'I will. I'll be vigilant,' I said, leaning in and hanging on his every word.

'If you see anything or anyone suspicious, you just let me know.'

I knew I should have been scared by all this but I was mostly flattered that Jamie seemed so concerned about me.

'I'm sorry if I'm a bit of a burden,' I said.

'Not at all. I'm sorry if I haven't always been here for you as much as I should have been. I'm not perfect. But I do realise how special you are and I do really like spending time with you.'

I couldn't concentrate on the rest of the conversation. My thoughts were racing ahead imagining the possibility that me and Jamie could actually be together. I hadn't let myself believe it could be a possibility until now.

Jamie asked me to meet him in the sports hall after college to practise my shifting, and of course I agreed without a moment's hesitation.

When I entered the sports hall Jamie was a lot frostier than he had been just a few hours earlier.

'I heard about the silly stunt you pulled earlier,' he said bluntly, his arms crossed over his chest.

He took me by surprise and I didn't know how to respond. 'It was just a bit of fun,' I said awkwardly.

'It was an unnecessary risk, that's what it was.' I guess I couldn't really argue with that. 'You could have been caught. This isn't a joke, Mollie. You should be practising your shifting with me in a controlled environment, at least at first. And the Drifters are a real threat. I suppose it's my fault for trying to protect you from the whole truth, but the Drifters are ruthless and dangerous. If they manage to take you back to their headquarters I don't know if we would be able to rescue you.'

I hate being told off. I looked down at my trainers and shuffled uncomfortably.

Jamie's expression began to soften a little as he beckoned me to the centre of the court to put me through my paces. We warmed up by running a couple of laps of the hall together. Neither of us said a word. Then we did a mixture of korfball skills and shifting, such as shifting into a different member of the korfball team between every pass.

'Clara!' Jamie shouted. 'Good! Now Will. Good! Now Amber. Faster! Good! Now Ed.'

The passes started slow but gradually sped up and I began to feel dizzy and disoriented. Jamie caught me in his strong arms before I crumbled to the ground and took him with me. We landed in a heap and our eyes locked together.

'I'm sorry I got mad with you Mollie, I just want to protect you,' Jamie said softly. 'And right now, I really want to kiss you.' I started to lean towards him but he looked uncomfortable. What was stopping him? He must have known that of course I wanted to kiss him too.

Suddenly it twigged. I was still shifted as Ed!

At that very moment actual Ed entered the sports hall.

'Hey guys, just came to see how you're getting on,' he said before stopping abruptly as he spotted me, as him, in Jamie's arms.

Jamie and I fell about on the floor laughing.

'Well, this is super weird, I'm going to leave you to it,' Ed said whilst backing quickly out of the door.

Once Jamie and I had caught our breath we climbed to our feet and I shifted back to myself and felt much more comfortable. I was disappointed I didn't get a kiss but the moment had passed.

We headed towards the changing rooms and Jamie said, 'I'll meet you out the front once we've changed and I'll walk you home.' I hoped that meant he wanted to spend more time with me rather than he was just trying to be a gentleman. 'And good work tonight,' he added.

I hurriedly got changed and sprayed myself generously with perfume then stepped out the front of the college. The air felt cool and there was barely any sunlight left. The college grounds were mostly empty at this time of night but I saw some movement over by the bike sheds. It was Jamie. But just as I was about to approach, I noticed he was with someone. I couldn't see their face behind Jamie but they were tall and slim and blonde. Amber. What was she still doing here? Before I could look away Jamie had his arms wrapped around Amber's shoulders. The next thing I knew, they were kissing.

My heart sank. Mere minutes ago he was talking about kissing me. And I believed him. Which, in hindsight, was stupid. Why would he have ever chosen me over beautiful Amber. Maybe he was a bit intrigued by me. But that didn't mean he wanted to be with me. I was angry at myself for getting my hopes up and angry at Jamie for leading me on. He knew I was in a vulnerable state after he told me I was essentially being hunted by a group of "ruthless and dangerous" shapeshifters.

I snuck quickly and quietly out of the college grounds to avoid any awkward confrontation and then began to stomp home. After a few minutes, I heard footsteps behind me. I snapped my head round to look but couldn't see anyone. I decided to take the slightly longer, but less deserted route home, just to be sure.

Once inside my house, I rushed straight upstairs to my room and sat on my bed, just staring at the floor. As much as I tried, I just couldn't get the image of Jamie and Amber out of my head. Mum poked her head round the door. She must have sensed something was up.

'Do you want to talk about it?' she asked, although I expect she already knew the answer.

'Not really.'

Mum sat down next to me on the bed anyway, clearly desperate to help me in any way she could. I always wished we had a more open relationship; maybe this was the time.

'It's just ...' I didn't really know where to start. 'It's just I've never really felt like I fit in, and then I thought that was changing but turns out I'm still the same old loser.'

Mum put her arm round me and said sincerely, 'Mollie you never have been and never will be a loser. Sure, you've always been a little different, but that's what makes you special. Embrace everything that makes you special and different and you can't go wrong.'

'Thanks Mum,' I said. I appreciated her trying to understand what I was going through.

Once Mum had left my room I sat on my desk chair and stared at my face in my mirror. What does Amber have that I don't have? Long blonde hair, fluttery eyelashes and strong cheekbones to name only a few. Suddenly it dawned on me. I thought about what Mum had said about embracing what makes me special and different. Well, that would be my human shifting abilities. And why stay in my very average human shell when I could be so much better? People use make-up and cosmetic procedures to improve their looks; what I planned to do was just a slightly more extreme version of that.

It was decided then. I was going to shift into a stunningly beautiful girl and have the life I had always dreamed of. I would be popular and desirable, and Jamie would be a distant memory. Sure, it wasn't the best thought out plan, but I could iron out the details later. All that mattered was I was going to be the best version of me and I was going to fit in for the first time in my life. Plus, arguably most importantly, the Drifters wouldn't be able to find me so I could take "being kidnapped" off my list of things to worry about.

I got ready for bed and fell asleep quickly, feeling content that my life was going to change for the better. All night I had vivid dreams about my new perfect life. What could possibly go wrong?

CHAPTER 9

THE REST OF the week I just kept my head down and tried to avoid people as much as possible. It was difficult to avoid Rose, though, since we were used to spending so much time together.

'Mollie!' Rose called out, spotting me from across the corridor. 'You've been difficult to track down recently. Do you want to come over to my house tonight? I can buy popcorn and we can find a cheesy film to watch?'

'I'm really sorry, Rose. I've got a lot of work on at the moment. I really am swamped.'

'Oh, okay then,' Rose said despondently. 'Tomorrow night, maybe?'

'Yeah, maybe.'

I think we both knew that that meant no. I did feel awful lying to Rose, but I needed to put my time and effort into planning my brilliant new life. Rose had made plenty of new college friends anyway, she wouldn't be alone.

That evening I sat down in front of my laptop and opened the application page for Tanglewood College. I remembered completing the form just a couple of years ago, full of hope, prior to all the craziness and disappointment this year had brought me so far.

Name:

Okay, first stumbling block. What should my new name be? Something pretty, but not too girly. Something mysterious, but not odd. My mind had gone blank as I stared out of my bedroom window into the back garden. The daisies on the overgrown lawn caught my eye. Daisy? I said the name out loud and it sounded good. I continued to scan the garden for inspiration. Daisy Shed? No. Daisy Fence? No. Daisy Spade? Hmm, that didn't sound so bad, and I had to move on as there were many more decisions to be made.

Address:

I decided to choose a generic sounding street name and hoped the admissions secretary wouldn't look into it too much. "12 Church Street" sounded as good an address as any.

There was a box where I had to give a reason for my mid-year transfer. I wrote something about my dad having to move around for his work.

Please upload a recent photograph.

Okay, well I guess it was time to think about my new look. I wanted my hair to be long to my mid-back, honey blonde with highlights and a natural wave. Eyes ocean blue with long thick eyelashes that don't need mascara. A petite nose. Bone structure like I should be on the cover of a fashion magazine. Plump red lips. I wanted long slender legs and sculpted arms. Tall but not too tall.

I was building up an image in my mind and getting ready to make the shift. I stood up and peered outside my door quickly to make sure Mum wasn't lurking. Then I stood in the middle of my room, closed my eyes and clenched my fists and imagined Daisy Spade, from her perfect head of hair to her dainty toes. I felt a familiar tingle travel through my body then opened my eyes and rushed to the mirror.

'I've done it!' I exclaimed, accidentally out loud.

I turned my perfectly manicured hands over in front of my face in disbelief. Then I put my face right up to the mirror to study my razor-sharp cheek bones.

'Sweetheart, it's dinner time!' I heard Mum's voice echo up the stairs. I just had time to snap a quick selfie on my phone and upload it to my application. The SUBMIT button was staring at me. My finger hovered over the mouse pad. Was this really such a good idea? Could I really pull off such a huge transformation? I could feel my heart quickening and pounding in my chest. I submitted the form before I had a chance to change my mind, then I rushed downstairs for dinner.

'Coming!' I called out from the top of the stairs. That's odd, my voice sounded different. Luckily, I realised I needed to shift back right before I reached the bottom of the stairs and came face to face with Mum.

'Ah, there you are Mollie. Now come and tell me all

about your day.'

✧   ✧   ✧

SOMEHOW I MADE it to the end of the week and late Friday afternoon I walked home from college as myself for the last time. I slowed my pace and took the time to feel the wind blowing in my hair. Part of me felt sad and anxious, but I was also excited to have a fresh start and to feel beautiful for once in my life.

What would I tell Rose and Matthew? I needed to let them know I wouldn't be around anymore but I knew they wouldn't buy any old excuse. I would also need to avoid them in my new form so they wouldn't suspect anything.

I started to compose a text;

Hi, I don't know how to say this but I need to go away for a while. A long while. I can't explain. Please respect that and don't try to contact me. Thank you so much for your friendship, it meant a lot xxx

A lump formed in my throat as I pressed send. I knew I would still see them around in my new form, but it wouldn't be the same. But I was sure that, overall, my life would be better. Once I am the beautiful Daisy Spade I will make loads of new friends and I will have the pick of all the guys in the college. Plus, no more worrying about the Drifters.

After sending the texts I put my phone on silent. I

knew Rose would try to phone me despite my pleas for her not to. There was no more Mollie. Daisy would need a new phone and a new number. I had already set up a new email address for the college to contact me about Daisy's application. I also emailed the college as Mollie to explain I would be leaving and made up an excuse about Mum needing to move at short notice for work. It was taking a lot of concentration to make sure I didn't mix up my two identities. Just as I was beginning to wonder again whether this was such a good idea after all, an email alert popped up on my phone;

Subject: Re college application

Dear Miss Spade

Thank you for your recent application. We do not usually have space to take new students mid-term but fortunately for you we have just received news of an opening. Please come to the main office at 9am Monday morning to meet with myself so we can go through some paperwork and get you acquainted with the college.

I look forward to meeting you.

Miss Maple
PA to Principal Golding

Well, I guessed there was no backing out now.

✧　✧　✧

MONDAY MORNING CAME around quickly. I had spent the

majority of the weekend in my room, flitting between a state of anxiety and excitement. Mum, as always, knew something was up, but I managed to keep her probing questions at bay by telling her I just wasn't feeling very well. Obviously I couldn't even begin to explain to her what was really going on.

I got ready for college as normal as I had decided it would be safer to shift once I was out of the house so Mum didn't catch me. I bounded downstairs and rushed into the kitchen to grab a quick breakfast.

'Morning, love. Are you feeling more like yourself again?' Mum was up already, still in her dressing gown and gripping a large cup of black coffee.

'Huh?' I responded, my heart skipping a beat.

'You said you weren't feeling well over the week-end …'

'Oh, that. Yes, I'm feeling much better, thanks. I think there was a bug going round at college.'

My stomach was doing somersaults but I poured myself some cereal to give me strength for the day ahead.

'I'm glad you're feeling better,' Mum said. 'I hope you're not pushing yourself too much at college and making yourself ill. You know I'm always proud of you, no matter what.'

'Yes, Mum. I know.'

I wolfed down the cereal then grabbed my bag and prepared to leave. But I turned at the front door and went back to give Mum a big hug.

'Oh!' Mum said. 'Thanks love. Have a nice day.'

I hurried towards college, knowing I needed some extra time to shift on the way. Around halfway into my journey I stepped off the path into a wooded area. I ventured a good way in to be safe, stepping over tree roots and crunchy leaves as I went. I closed my eyes and imagined Daisy Spade. A tingle started in the top of my head and ran right down to my toes. I opened my eyes and looked down at my slender fingers and long manicured nails. I reached into my bag, pulled out my compact mirror and flipped it open. A sigh of relief escaped my plump lips. Perfect.

My stomach continued to do somersaults all the way to college. In fact, it felt like it was doing a full gymnastic floor routine.

I walked nervously up the stone steps and through the large front doors. I took some comfort in the familiarity of the building. I turned left and headed towards Miss Maple's office. I had met her only a couple of times before. She was friendly enough but I hoped that today she wouldn't ask me too many questions. I had been practising saying my new details like date of birth and address but it still didn't come naturally, especially under pressure.

Knock knock.

'Come in!' I heard a sing-song voice through the door.

This was it. Last chance to run. I grasped the cold

metal door handle with a trembling hand, opened the door slightly and popped my head through. The office was a little messy to say the least and Miss Maple was standing by her desk flicking through a large pile of papers. She had frizzy blonde hair and black rectangular glasses perched on the end of her nose.

'Hello!' she said. 'And who might you be?'

The blood drained from my face. Had I not shifted correctly? Should I just run away?

'Hello,' I replied. 'I'm, uh, Daisy. Daisy Spade?' I didn't mean for it to sound like a question.

'Daisy Spade? Daisy Spade? Where do I know that name? Oh, of course, you're our new student. Welcome. Sorry, the beginning of the week is always a bit hectic.'

I smiled and my heart rate began to slow back to normal as I entered the room, carefully stepping over a strewn hole puncher and stapler as I approached Miss Maple's desk.

She started to search through another towering pile of papers.

'Ah ha!' It appeared she had found my documents. 'Come, take a seat.'

That was easier said than done in amongst all the clutter.

'I am Miss Maple, PA to Principal Golding. This meeting is to confirm all your details and to get to know a bit more about you. So, no difficult questions, I promise!'

If only she knew. I twisted my long hair round my

fingers and looked down at the floor.

'Firstly, can you confirm your address for me please?'

'Yes it's um, yes, um …'

Ring ring, ring ring.

'Sorry, excuse me just a moment, Daisy.'

Miss Maple tossed most of the contents of her desk onto the floor whilst trying to locate her phone. Eventually she managed to pick up the receiver and put it to her ear. 'Yes? Sorry I mean, this is Miss Maple, PA to Principal … Oh, hello Principal Golding. No, of course I haven't forgotten. I'll be with you right away.'

Miss Maple's face dropped. 'I'm so sorry, I've double booked. I'm meant to be helping Principal Golding with a new teacher interview.'

'It's really no problem,' I said, relief washing over me.

'Well, you need to be given a tour at least. Let me see what I can do.'

'Really, don't worry. I can find my own way around.' My protest fell on deaf ears as Miss Maple leapt from her seat and popped her head round the door, searching up and down the corridor.

'Hey, you! Yes, you,' I heard her shout, 'Michael, is it? Oh yes, sorry. I have a favour to ask. Could you please give our new student a quick tour? Yes, don't worry. I'll explain to Miss Hawkins why you're late.' She was almost pleading with the mystery student now. 'Ah, brilliant. You're a star.' Miss Maple let out a sigh and beckoned me over to the door. 'Daisy, this is Matthew. He will be your tour guide.' And with that, she scarpered away down the hall.

Matthew. Oh dear. My fingers started to tingle and it took all my strength to maintain my composure.

You are not awkward Mollie anymore. You are beautiful, confident Daisy.

'Nice to meet you, I'm Daisy,' I said extending my hand. But Matthew had already turned to walk ahead of me.

'Follow me, we'll make it quick,' he said. 'On the left you've got the science labs. Here on the right are the rooms for English and history.' I had to take long strides with my new legs to keep up with him. I wished I had worn more sensible shoes. 'Straight ahead is the canteen; the fish on Fridays is good otherwise I would advise you bring in your own lunch.' I tried to act like this was the first time I had seen the college, although Matthew was barely taking any notice of me anyway. We went out the back entrance and Matthew pointed across the courtyard to show me the sports hall.

'And that's about it,' he said matter-of-factly.

I just stared at him, not quite knowing what to say.

'I'm sorry,' he said, shaking his head. His blonde fringe flopped over his eyes. 'It's just, I've got a lot going on. The girl who's spot you have taken, well, she was my friend and—'

'Do you want to eat lunch together and talk about it?' I blurted out without really thinking. This wasn't part of my plan at all but seeing Matthew again, and looking so sad, I just wanted to spend time with him. I took the opportunity to practise my flirting and fluttered my new long eyelashes.

'Um, oh, uh,' Matthew shuffled awkwardly. Had I fluttered too much? 'Sorry, I can't. I mean, I could but, well, I've just got a lot on my mind. I wouldn't be very good company.'

He looked down at the floor and scuttled off shouting, 'Good luck with your first day!' over his shoulder.

Ouch. Although I knew it was for the best that I didn't spend more time with Matthew, it didn't make his rejection hurt any less.

I made it through my morning classes and couldn't wait to escape to get something to eat. The corridors were busy as usual at this time of day. But something felt different as I walked down them towards the canteen. Were people staring at me? Had I tucked my skirt into my underwear? A quick tug on my skirt revealed I was okay. Then I realised, maybe it was just Daisy they were staring at. The hot new student. People were staring at me and it wasn't because I had done something stupid. I couldn't quite believe it. As my confidence grew, my usual shuffle turned into more of a strut.

'Uh, excuse me, uh, hi.' Another student stopped me in the corridor with his deep masculine voice. I recognised him as Dan, captain of the football team. 'You're really fit,' he said, gawping at me.

'Oh, uh, thanks,' I blushed. I definitely could have said the same about him, but I decided to play it cool.

'It's my first day here,' I said. 'I'm just trying to find my feet.'

'Yeah, 'course, I would've remembered someone as pretty as you if you'd been here before.'

'Thanks … again. So, do you like it here? Is it a good college?' I liked the fact Dan wanted to talk to me; he never would have even looked in my direction before. But so far he didn't really have much to say for himself.

'Uh, yeah, it's good.' He wasn't making eye contact, choosing to focus slightly lower. 'So, uh, do you want to hang tonight?'

Only half a day in and I had already secured a date!

'Oh, um, sure. What were you thinking? A café, the cinema, a park?'

'Or I could take you back to my house on my motorbike and we could just hang.' He still wasn't making eye contact and I was starting to feel a bit uneasy.

'You know what, I'll need to check my schedule,' I replied as I hurried away down the corridor. I nearly tripped over my new feet in my rush to escape but managed to steady myself against the wall.

I reached the canteen and it felt like my very first day all over again. I spotted Rose sat on a table in the corner with her dance friends and my whole body ached to go over to her and give her a hug. I could feel my eyes starting to fill with tears so walked the other way.

'Hello there.' I heard a familiar voice and it made the hair on my arms stand on end. Amber. 'Would you like to sit with us?' she asked in a sickly-sweet voice.

I looked around, not quite believing she was talking me.

'Yes you, silly,' she said. 'I love your hair. You must tell me how you get it so shiny.'

I flashed Amber a half-smile but involuntarily looked over towards Rose again.

Amber clearly noticed. 'Oh, you don't want to sit with *her*; she's a nobody.'

Rose must have heard as she looked round at Amber and rolled her eyes. Good for her. I hesitated for a second and felt sick to my stomach but I couldn't just go back to my old life.

I took my bag off my shoulder and sat down on a seat opposite Amber and said confidently, 'Hi, I'm Daisy.'

'Hi Daisy. I'm Amber, and this is Clara and Emma.' Amber tilted her head and studied my face. 'You have a perfectly symmetrical face, did you know that? So pretty. I have no cheek bones. I need to get fillers.'

'No way, you're so naturally pretty,' I blurted out. Although she could be mean, no one could deny her beauty.

'Why, thank you,' she replied, before turning her head to look at Clara and Emma in turn.

'Oh yes, so pretty,' they both agreed, nodding their

heads vigorously.

'So, straight to the important stuff. Have any guys here caught your eye yet?'

'Well this guy called Dan started chatting to me in the corridor and I think he asked me out on a date this evening.'

'Oooh,' Clara and Emma said in unison.

'Wait, wait,' Amber interrupted. 'Football captain Dan? Did he invite you on an actual date or did he invite you to "hang" at his house?'

'How did you know?' I asked.

'Daisy, he is after one thing and one thing only. He got himself a bit of a reputation and now any girl with an ounce of self-respect won't go near him.'

Emma quickly piped up, 'Hey! I hung out with him last week!'

Amber shot Emma a disapproving look.

'He's hot …' Emma said sheepishly.

Amber continued, 'Daisy, and apparently you too Emma, have much to learn about this college. We should have a girl's night at mine tonight for a proper gossip.'

As much as I didn't like to admit it, I think I needed Amber to teach me the ropes of being popular. It didn't mean I had to like her. I could just pretend until I had learned enough to survive on my own. I could do that. I think.

'Sure,' I replied. 'Sounds like fun.'

'Fabulous!' Amber smiled, showing off her impossibly white teeth.

And just like that, I was one of the popular girls.

CHAPTER 10

AMBER TEXTED ME her address later in the afternoon and I instantly recognised the road name: Highfield Drive. It was a road full of huge, posh houses with electric gates and beautifully manicured front gardens. I had always wondered what they were like inside. I made my way there after my last class, although my legs felt weary and all I really wanted was to have a shower and crawl into bed.

Number thirty-five. I had found it. I looked around to see if there was a bell of some sort but the iron gates opened automatically. I walked up the gravel driveway, past a fleet of shiny, expensive-looking cars. Amber was already standing at the grand front door waving and Emma and Clara were standing just behind her.

'Daisy, hi. So glad you made it. Come on in,' Amber called out.

I stepped into the hallway and looked around. It was very fancy. And white. And immaculately clean. There were lots of ornaments balanced delicately on tables and shelves and I made a mental note not to touch anything.

It felt very different to my house. Not least the pictures on the wall; here there were paintings of scenery or historical figures, whereas at home Mum had hung up all my childhood photos (including some embarrassing ones that I constantly beg her to take down).

'Come on, let's go to the kitchen and make a snack,' Amber said, heading towards one of the many doors leading off the grand hallway.

'Don't touch anything,' Clara helpfully whispered in my ear, and I vigorously nodded in response.

As I expected, the kitchen was massive and impeccably decorated. Lots of marble worktops and a large island in the middle. And at the island, perched on a stool, was a woman who was instantly recognisable as Amber's mum. She had short dark hair and thin lips, red with lipstick. She was wearing a black suit and typing away on her laptop intensely.

'Hello, Mother,' Amber said, before heading towards the shiny silver fridge freezer with inbuilt ice machine. Fancy.

'Cheese toastie?' Amber asked Emma, Clara and myself.

Before we could reply Amber's mother chimed in, 'Amber darling, cheese is very fattening. Why don't you try a piece of fruit instead.'

Amber just looked down at the tiled floor despondently and made her way to the sink to make us all drinks instead.

I noticed Amber's mum hadn't even said hello to us, I hoped she didn't mind us being in her amazing house.

'I got an A in music today,' Amber told her mum.

'Well, that's hardly going to get you into law school now, is it dear?'

'But I've told you, I don't want to go to law school like you!' Amber stuck her bottom lip out and roughly shoved ice cubes into the glasses.

'Now's not the time, Amber dear,' her mum said through gritted teeth, barely looking up from her laptop, her fingers continuing to tap away with speed.

I couldn't help but feel a bit sorry for Amber. Whenever Rose came over to my house, Mum would buzz around offering snacks and asking intrusive questions, but at least it showed she cared.

Amber led us up the spiral staircase to her bedroom and I was glad to get away from the frosty atmosphere.

Amber's room was as I had imagined it, styled to perfection. The large four poster bed was almost completely covered in decorative pillows. By the window was a dressing table with a large ornate mirror. There was even an ensuite bathroom. Amber probably didn't even appreciate just how lucky she was.

Amber threw some of her many pillows on the floor and sat down on her bed with a sigh. 'I miss my dad,' she said.

'Where is he?' I asked.

'He lives a couple of hours away with his new girlfriend who is fifteen years younger than him. Gross. Mum and Dad got divorced five years ago. Dad moved on pretty quickly. Mum never has and she's become terribly bitter. She never used to be so ...'

'Mean?' Emma interjected.

'Cold?' Clara offered.

'Yeah,' Amber said sadly.

I had never seen Amber so vulnerable before. However, it didn't last long as she quickly snapped out of it and changed the subject. 'Okay, Daisy. I need to talk about something personal so I need you to be in the circle of trust.'

'Okaaay,' I said, unsure exactly what I was getting myself into.

'Swear you won't share anything outside of this circle.'

'Okay, sure.'

'No, you have to swear.'

All three girls looked at me expectantly, waiting for me to complete their bizarre ritual. 'Okay ... I swear,' I said whilst trying not to roll my eyes.

'Good. So, I wanted to let you girls know ... me and Jamie kissed!'

'What?!' exclaimed Emma and Clara in unison.

'You're always so on and off, but I thought you were "off" at the moment?' Clara asked.

'I thought so too,' Amber replied. 'But last week I was getting my bike from the bike shed one evening when

Jamie came over out of nowhere and kissed me.'

I tried to keep a straight face. This was the last thing I wanted to be talking to Amber about.

'So what's happening now?' Emma asked.

'Well, that's the thing,' said Amber. 'He hasn't really spoken to me since. It's like the kiss never happened.'

'Maybe he regrets it,' I said casually. I couldn't help it, it just slipped out.

Luckily Amber didn't seem to have heard me. She was too lost in her own thoughts.

'What should I do?' Amber asked.

She was looking at me. I froze. I couldn't do this anymore. It was a silly idea trying to befriend Amber when she was half the reason I was in this situation.

'Uh, actually I don't feel too well,' I said standing up, clutching my stomach for effect.

'Well whatever you do don't puke on the cream carpet, Mum would kill us all!' Amber said. 'Clara, show her out please. Quickly!'

Clara obediently jumped to her feet and guided me out into the hallway.

'I hope you feel better,' Amber called out as an afterthought.

I hurried down the driveway and headed home. It was dark apart from the glow of the street lights. Luckily, it wasn't too cold as I hadn't thought to bring a coat. Girls' night really hadn't gone as planned. But tomorrow was a new day.

'Alright love!' I heard a deep voice shout from behind me, followed by another man laughing. I carried on walking, hoping they weren't talking to me.

'Nice legs!' I heard, followed by more laughter. My pace quickened.

'We're headed to a party. Wanna join?'

This time I turned around. I saw two guys, probably a couple of years older than me. They looked quite scruffy in jeans and trainers and one of them was smoking.

'No thank you, I'm just on my way home,' I said, way more politely than they deserved.

'Aww, come on sexy. It'll be fun.'

Wow, they do not give up. Although my heart was pumping hard in my chest and adrenaline was coursing through my veins, I had an idea. I ran off up a side road so I was out of view and quickly shifted before walking back out on to the main street. But not as Daisy, as a tall, muscular, intimidating man.

'Uh, excuse me, mate,' one of the guys said to me. 'Did you see a fit girl run off down there?'

'She's my girlfriend,' I replied in a deep voice. 'Leave her alone; she's not interested.'

'Ah mate, we're really sorry. We didn't realise she had a boyfriend. You're a lucky man. Have a good night, mate.'

And with that, they staggered off.

I walked most of the rest of the way home shifted as a man to avoid any more uncomfortable situations. All I could think about was how sad it was that those guys didn't respect me as a woman when I said no, yet they respected another man without question. I tried not to think about what might have happened if I didn't have the ability to shift.

✧   ✧   ✧

FOLLOWING MY ABRUPT and slightly embarrassing departure from her house, Amber was less keen to befriend me anymore. When I walked into the canteen at lunchtimes she would concentrate on pushing her salad round her plate and pretend she hadn't seen me. Meanwhile, Clara and Emma would sneak a glance at me and smile apologetically. Football captain Dan, on the other hand, had remained very keen. I kept bumping into him in the corridor and I began to realise it wasn't always an accident.

'Are you following me?' I asked with a smile.

'Maybe our good looks just draw us together,' Dan replied.

'So cheesy!'

'Huh?'

Oops, I hadn't meant to say that out loud. Quick, say something to distract him. I just smiled and fluttered my eyelashes, which seemed to do the trick.

'Come and watch my football match tonight?' he asked. 'It's our biggest match of the season. There should be quite a crowd. All the team's girlfriends are watching together. I can introduce you … Uh, not that you're my girlfriend … uh, unless you want to be?'

I had discovered during our brief encounters that Dan was nice enough, if a little vain, but I certainly didn't know enough about him to be his girlfriend.

'I think we're moving a little too fast, Dan,' I said as his face dropped and he glanced behind him, likely to check than none of his mates could overhear him being rejected. 'But I'd be happy to come and watch you play football tonight.' I didn't mind football as a sport and besides, I could do with making some new girl friends.

'Great, I'll see you there at six o'clock,' Dan said as he strolled off with his usual confident swagger.

I still had to pinch myself that I was being pursued by someone like Dan.

When I got to the football pitch after college they had set up some tiered seating along one side of the pitch and it was around half full. Not a bad set up and turn out for a college match. I spotted Dan warming up. He looked athletic in his kit and full of energy. When he spotted me he came running over.

'Hey!' he panted. His fringe was stuck to his forehead with sweat but he still looked good. He pulled off his navy-blue training jacket and placed it over my shoulders. 'The girls are up there at the back,' he said pointing. I saw four girls sat also wearing training jackets like the one that had just been thrust upon me. 'Just go up there and say hi,' he said, clearly unaware of how anxious I felt about meeting new people.

But I was Daisy now. Beautiful, confident, popular Daisy. I could do this.

'Good luck,' I called as he ran back on to the pitch to continue his warm up.

I took a deep breath and headed towards the girls at the back of the stand who were chatting away animatedly.

'Excuse me, hi, I'm Daisy,' I said.

'Oh hi, Daisy,' they replied in unison. Then the girl nearest to me said, 'I'm Jessica, and this is Alice, Isobel and Hayley. Welcome to the WAGs!'

'Oh, well, me and Dan, we're just friends,' I said, unconvincingly.

'He's a very good-looking guy,' Isobel said. 'Just, well, not a lot going on upstairs.' The other girls giggled. 'Not like my Harry,' she continued. 'He's top scorer and he's going to be a lawyer.'

'Oh my god, you're going to be, like, so rich,' Hayley said, looking jealous.

'Anyway, sit down, Daisy,' Jessica said, patting the red plastic seat next to her.

'Do you want a swig?' Alice asked, leaning over with a hip flask in her hand.

'Oh no, I'm okay thank you,' I replied, the memory of the Battle of the Bands night replaying in my head.

'We don't really pay much attention to the match,' Alice said, although I had already guessed as much. 'We make sure we watch just enough so we can stroke our boys' egos after the match, but otherwise it's just a great time for a gossip.'

I smiled then zoned out for a bit whilst they continued to talk about how rich they would be once their other halves made it as Premier League footballers. A few rows down, I spotted the Shifters, obviously taking a rare evening off from korfball training or shifting practice. I missed Ed's curly hair and his wicked sense of humour. I missed Ava and her down-to-earth approach to life. Most of all, I missed Matthew's kind smile and his loyal friendship. I could see Jamie sat next to Amber. I wasn't sure how I felt about him but he still made the hairs on my arms stand on end.

'Daisy, it's great that you're here and we would love to welcome you into the group, but, well, we need to know that you're cool,' Jessica said, pulling me back to their conversation. 'We need to know we can trust you with all our secrets.' They obviously hadn't realised I hadn't been listening to a word they had said anyway.

'Yeah, sure,' I said.

Jessica looked around the stand. 'Ah,' she finally said. 'Look down there to our right, the dance weirdos are here. See that girl in the hideous multi-coloured jumper?' I felt sick, as before I even looked up, I knew who she was talking about. Rose. She was sat on the aisle, talking to Jenny and the rest of her dance friends, minding her own business. What did Jessica want with her? Jessica continued, 'Take my cup of Coke, walk down there and as you pass "accidentally" trip and spill the drink down her stupid jumper.'

'But why?' I asked, my nausea building.

The girls all shrugged. 'Because it's funny,' Alice said matter-of-factly.

'I don't think so. I think it's just mean,' I said. I wanted to be popular, but not at this cost.

'Well, if you don't do it, I will,' Hayley piped up.

Jessica thrust her cup of Coke and ice into my hand. Her stare was threatening. I stood up and my legs felt like jelly. What was I going to do?

I started walking gingerly down the steps, my heart rate quickening, until I was standing just behind Rose. There was no way I was doing it. I looked up at the girls and shook my head but at that point I realised Hayley was already bounding down the steps towards me. A couple of seconds later, she lurched towards me and tried to knock the cup out of my hand and onto Rose, but I reacted by gripping it tighter and pulling the cup the other way, which resulted in the drink going all over me.

'Ah!' I yelped, from the shock of what had happened and the shock of the ice cube that had found its way into my bra.

Hayley just scowled at me and marched back to the WAGs, leaving me standing there alone with people pointing and laughing.

I glanced at Rose and she looked concerned but also utterly confused as to what had just happened. At least she was dry, that was the main thing.

I hurried the rest of the way down the stand and back along the edge of the football pitch.

'Hey, where are you going?' Dan had spotted me. 'Oh,' he said, noticing the Coke stains all down my front, 'What happened? Are you okay?'

'Well not really, but—'

'Uh,' he interrupted. 'Is that a stain on my training jacket?' His nostrils flared as he stared at the large brown stain on the shoulder of his jacket. Suddenly, whether or not I was okay was no longer his biggest concern.

I shrugged off the stupid ugly jacket and threw it on the floor at his feet before storming off.

'Hey, Daisy,' he called out after me and I turned around to see what he had to say for himself. 'Would you mind washing that for me?'

I was too angry to even think of a reply that wasn't mostly swear words. He wasn't worth my breath.

I stomped home, wet, cold and humiliated. All I wanted was to curl up with a hot chocolate in my warm bed. I was nearly home when I spotted Rose's brother, Jake, walking towards me. He was out walking Milo. When Milo spotted me, his tail started wagging and he came bounding over as fast as he could, pulling hard against his lead and forcing Jake to break into a jog.

'Milo!' I called out, crouching down to give him a stroke. This was just the animal therapy I needed.

'Hi,' Rose's brother said as he got nearer. 'Do you

know Milo?'

'Oh, yes, I'm a friend of Rose's. I'm Mol—. I'm Daisy. Daisy.'

'Nice to meet you, Daisy. I'm Jake. Milo has always been the friendliest dog.'

Just as he said that, Milo backed up away from me with his back arched. He bared his sharp canines and growled.

'It's okay, Milo,' I said gently, offering out a hand.

Then Milo started barking madly and he wouldn't stop. In the end, Jake had to drag him away. He looked mortified.

'I'm so sorry,' he mouthed over his shoulder. 'I don't know what's come over him.'

CHAPTER 11

S O, I HAD managed to alienate myself from all the popular groups at college and even Milo hated me. I spent most of my days just going to my classes and eating alone. Except for the occasional times guys would strike up conversations with me. Or, more accurately, gawp at me, tell me I'm pretty then have nothing more to say for themselves. I had even had to endure a few cheesy chat-up lines. 'I seem to have lost my phone number. Can I have yours?' and my personal least favourite, 'Are you a parking ticket? 'Cause you've got fine written all over you.' How was I even meant to respond to that?

One sunny lunch time I decided to eat outside on a wooden bench in a quiet corner of the playing field. It wasn't particularly warm but it was better than being alone in the crowded café or hidden in a toilet stall. I tilted my head back, closed my eyes and concentrated on the sounds of the birds. This meant I didn't notice anyone approaching until they sat down beside me. I opened my eyes and jerked my head to the left to see who was guilty of disturbing my peaceful moment. It was one of the most beautiful men I had ever seen. And this was definitely a man, not a college guy. He looked older, in his thirties I guessed. He just sat there staring straight ahead, unblinking. I realised I had been gawping at his perfect features so turned to look straight ahead as well.

After a minute or two he finally spoke.

'I know who you are,' he said, still looking straight ahead. His voice was deep and silky. The hairs on the back of my neck stood on end and my muscles tightened.

'Well I'm afraid I have no idea who you are,' I replied, trying to keep the fear from entering my voice.

'My name is Archer. Nice to meet you ... Mollie Thomas.' He emphasised my name. My old name. It felt strange to be called it again. And more importantly how on earth did he know?

'Uh, I think you're mistaken. My name is Daisy, and I really must be going,' I said, getting up to leave. My legs were shaking.

Archer didn't move a muscle. He simply said, 'Mollie, I am a shapeshifter too, just like you. Trust me, you're going to want to hear what I have to say.'

My whole body froze. He was a Drifter. My body was telling me to run away but something deep inside me wanted to hear what he had to say.

'You're a Drifter?' I asked, my eyes scanning over his perfect facial features.

'I certainly am,' he said.

'How did you find me?' My body could only produce

a whisper.

'We're all connected, Mollie. Especially gifted shapeshifters like us. It was really only ever a matter of time before we found you. You have so much to learn. The Drifters can teach you everything you need to know.'

'The Drifters are liars and thieves,' I said. I managed to look him right in his eyes but the tremble in my voice gave away how I was really feeling.

Archer smiled gently. 'Mollie, there are some things you need to understand. Humans will never accept us into their society. They are too scared of anything different to themselves. So we have to forge our own way in the world. We don't hurt people if we don't have to. It's not our fault humans are so narrow-minded and intolerant. Don't you want to be the best person you can be? You are very, very special, Mollie.'

Archer's voice was mesmerising. And some of what he was saying was making sense.

'I do want to be the best person I can be,' I said.

'Then join us, Mollie. Fulfil your true destiny. We need someone as young and talented as you for our biggest mission yet. Five years ago, when we went to the human government all we asked for was acceptance and equality but we were denied that. So now we are going to take control. Mollie, tell me, who is the most powerful person in England?'

'The Queen?'

'A common misconception, but no, it's the Prime

Minister. We need you to shift into the Prime Minister so we can take control of the country. As we get older it becomes harder to hold a transformation for a prolonged period of time but you can do it. The rest of the Drifters would gradually infiltrate the government to support you and eventually we can pass whatever laws we like.' He paused, then looked directly into my eyes. 'We would have complete control.'

I laughed involuntarily. 'You're joking, right?'

'No, deadly serious,' Archer said in a low voice. 'The humans think they can silence us. Ha! They have no idea what they're up against. You should join the Drifters and fulfil your destiny.' He leaned in towards me and his spicy aftershave filled my nostrils. 'You're very special Mollie.'

'So you said. But the Shifters strongly disagree with the things you do.'

Archer let out an irritated sigh. 'Of course they do. They are jealous too. And who could blame them when they can only turn into animals. Useless!' He chuckled to himself then looked me straight in the eyes again. 'Mollie, you will never fit in with the humans or the Shifters. You need to join us. Fulfil your destiny.'

I wanted to shout at him, 'I control my own destiny!' but thought I needed to choose my words carefully to get out of this situation safely.

When Archer called me special it was intoxicating and it was so tempting to explore a world where I was special and wanted. But the rational side of my brain knew he was grooming me and I knew the Drifters were not good people.

'Your proposition is very interesting. I hope you understand though that I will need some time to think it over,' I said, as calmly as I could manage.

'Our leader, Mr Silverman, is not a very patient man,' Archer replied coldly. 'I can grant you some time, although I don't quite understand what there is to think about. Fulfil your destiny Mollie.'

Alright already!

'How much time do I have?' I asked, but Archer had already slinked away as quickly and quietly as he had appeared.

A shiver ran down my spine and I just sat silently for the rest of my lunch break, no longer able to stomach my food.

I couldn't concentrate on my afternoon lessons at all. All I could hear was Archer's voice going round and round in my head, '*Fulfil your destiny Mollie.*' When the final bell went, I strode down the corridor towards the front exit as quickly as Daisy's legs could carry me. I spotted Dan chatting to a group of pretty girls by the lockers.

'Yo, Daisy! Hey, gorgeous! Don't walk away. Can't we just talk?'

Dan was the last person I wanted to talk to right now so I just kept walking without a further look in his direction. I wasn't interested in anything he had to say. I walked out the front of the college, leapt down the steps and made my way home. As my shoes pounded against the pavement, I gradually started to feel like I could breathe again. I walked and walked and walked. I just wanted to get away. Anywhere.

I eventually stopped and realised I had walked right past my house. I had come to the edge of some woodland. I ventured inside a bit. It was quiet and calm. No noise, no distractions, no people, no judgement. I rested my hand against a tree trunk to catch my breath and tears started rolling down my cheeks. They wouldn't stop. I felt so stupid. This whole thing had been an awful idea. I had abandoned my friends in pursuit of perfection but on reflection my life had already been pretty perfect. I was just too stupid and shallow to see it. So stupid.

A rustling in the trees snapped me out of my pity party.

'Hello?' I called whilst wiping the salty tears from my cheeks with my hands.

Nothing.

I was probably just jumpy after today's events. Even so, I wanted to get out of these woods as quickly as possible.

I leaned my back against the cold hard bark of the tree, closed my eyes and relaxed so I could shift back to my normal self. I had gotten pretty good at it and Mum hadn't suspected a thing this whole time.

Another rustle. Closer this time. Then a flash of blue eyes. Heavy breathing. A snap of a twig. I quickly flicked my head from side to side, trying to locate the source of the noises. Then a grey wolf strode out from behind a nearby bush. But it was only there for a second before it shifted into…

'Matthew! Uh, how long have you been there?' I couldn't stop my voice from shaking.

'Long enough,' he replied.

'I can explain.'

'No, me first.' I could sense the emotion in his voice so just stood still and listened. 'We need you back Mollie. I need you back. I don't know exactly what this was all about, but we can work it out. We need to protect you from the Drifters and—'

'I met one,' I interrupted.

'You did?' Matthew asked, his eyes widening. 'Are you okay?'

'Yes, I'm fine. He wanted me to join them. He said I was special.'

'You are special, Mollie. But you should use your ability for good, not for the twisted agenda of the Drifters. I know your life has been turned upside down recently and maybe we haven't been supportive enough, but just tell me what I can do. I'll do anything.'

I ran over to him and fell into his arms. It felt so good. We just stood there, embracing, for what felt like hours.

'You didn't need to say all that,' I said breaking the silence.

'But I need to convince you to come back,' Matthew said earnestly.

I smiled. 'No, you don't. I had already made up my mind. I know I made a huge mistake. I just didn't know how to make it right. I'm so embarrassed. All this, just because I saw Jamie kissing Amber.'

'Err, no he didn't. Amber was saying the same thing and they got into a huge argument about it. But then we realised Amber had no reason to lie and we figured it must have been a Drifter shifted as Jamie. We couldn't work out why though, but now it all makes sense. They must have planned it to push you away from us and towards them.'

'So Jamie didn't kiss Amber?'

'No,' Matthew said, sounding mildly irritated that I was focussing on that.

'You're right, it doesn't matter. I just can't believe this was all part of their plan.'

'We need to tell the others that a Drifter approached you. It won't be long before they show up again.'

'Agreed. But, can I just ask, how did you know I was Daisy?'

'Well, it was a few things actually. The way Daisy walked a little clumsily, the way her eyes lit up when she smiled, the way she appeared confident but was clearly anxious underneath.' Matthew looked down at the ground and shuffled his feet. 'The others didn't believe me, they thought I was mad, so I decided to follow you home to see if I was right.'

'Well I'm very glad you did,' I said, giving him another hug.

CHAPTER 12

I MANAGED TO enrol myself back into Tanglewood College. I think Miss Maple was thoroughly confused with the whole situation but luckily she was too busy trying to get herself organised to ask too many questions.

The Shifters had arranged to meet on the sports field after college on my first day back. I was excited, but nervous to see them all again. As I walked towards the field it appeared I was the last one to arrive.

Ava came running over and threw her arms around me. 'Mollie! I'm so glad you're back. We thought the Drifters had taken you!' she said.

'Don't ever leave us again please,' Ed chimed in with a smile. 'We all missed you. And Matthew has just moped around and not smiled once the whole time you've been gone!'

Ed gave Matthew a friendly poke in the ribs with his elbow but Matthew just gave him a warning look. And was he blushing a little bit?

Amber, Clara and Emma were sitting slightly apart from the group and barely looked at me. But then, as I was having a catch up with Will, Amber marched over and dragged me away roughly by the arm.

'You had better not say anything,' she hissed at me, barely an inch from my face.

'About what?' I asked, genuinely perplexed.

'About my home life. And my mum.'

I felt upset that she actually thought I would use that against her.

'Amber, I promise I won't say a word. And I'm always here if you ever want to talk—'

'Ugh,' she said turning to walk away, 'I do not want to talk to you.'

I couldn't blame her I guess. I did lie to her. And to everyone else.

Jamie came strolling over to me with his hands in his coat pockets. 'Hey,' was all he said.

'Hey.' I didn't know where to start. It felt like a lifetime since we had last spoken.

'I'm sorry,' we both said in unison.

We both laughed and I could feel the tension lifting slightly.

'I'm just glad you're okay,' Jamie said, placing his hand on my arm.

'I certainly learned a few lessons. Like it's hard pretending to be someone you're not. Really hard.'

'Well, I for one, am glad Mollie is back.'

'Thanks. Not everyone is glad though,' I said, gesturing towards Amber.

'Give her time, she'll come round. And by the way, nothing happened between me and Amber.'

'I know,' I said looking down at my muddy boots.

'I couldn't believe it when Matthew told me you had been approached by a Drifter. I told my dad and he said we all need to be extra vigilant and look out for you. He's still working on the anti-shifting serum. He says we need to hold the Drifters off until he has perfected it to the right potency.'

'I'm honestly fine. For once I am happy with who I am and I'm not going to let the Drifters ruin that. But thanks for looking out for me.' It was nice to know that Jamie, and the rest of the Shifters, cared about me.

'You're tougher than you think you are, Mollie. Now let's join the others. Ed brought us all snacks.'

We all sat in a circle on the field watching the sun set and munching on crisps and popcorn. I sat next to Matthew for a catch up and we shared a blanket to keep warm.

'Maths was rubbish without you,' he said. 'I had no one to talk to and help me with trigonometry. Miss Hawkins even made me stay behind one evening for extra tutoring!'

'I'm sorry I abandoned you. I'll help you get back up to speed, I promise.'

'So, are you going to continue to pursue the lovely Dan?' Matthew asked with a grin.

'Ugh, no,' I said. 'That was a big mistake. Daisy might have put up with him for a bit but Mollie is not interested in the slightest!'

'Well, I'm glad Mollie has better judgement than Daisy.'

'You didn't like Daisy, did you?' I asked. 'You were pretty cold when you were asked to show her round college on her first day.'

'Yeah, sorry about that. She just didn't look like someone I would be friends with. I guess I'm also guilty of judging people by their looks.' Matthew continued to steal my popcorn as he added, 'In my defence, I had also just lost my best friend.'

'Aww, best friend? Shall I buy us matching friendship bracelets?' I joked.

When we stopped laughing I realised everything had gone quiet. Even the birds had stopped chirping and it felt like the temperature had suddenly dropped.

Approaching fast from the other side of the field was a figure I recognised. A strikingly beautiful figure of a man who sent shivers down my spine. I could see the other Shifters look between Archer and myself and from my tense reaction they seemed to put two and two together.

Everyone stood up and formed a protective semi-circle around me, even Amber. Jamie and Matthew were stood at the front.

'Leave right now, Drifter. Mollie doesn't want to talk to you,' Jamie growled.

'How rude; I haven't even introduced myself. I am Archer, and I have been sent by my leader, Mr Silverman.'

Jamie just continued to stare him down and puffed out his chest. Archer didn't appear at all intimidated.

'No need to introduce yourselves,' Archer continued. 'I've done my homework and I know who you all are. Would you like a saucer of milk, *cat boy*?'

Jamie's fists clenched.

I couldn't let them fight for me and I didn't want anyone to get hurt. I pushed forward between Jamie and Matthew. They tried to grab my arms to pull me back but I shrugged them off.

'Ah,' Archer smiled, 'I assume you have come to your senses and decided to join us. Finally, you will have the chance to fulfil your destiny, Mollie.'

'No!' I shouted at a volume which even took me by surprise. 'I know what my destiny is. I am a Shifter, not a Drifter. I am a good person. Humans are good people. I want to live alongside them, not take advantage of them and hurt them. So leave me and my friends alone.'

That felt good. Archer strode towards me menacingly, but thanks to the adrenaline coursing through my veins I didn't back down.

'I've tried really hard to be nice,' Archer said through

gritted teeth. 'Really hard. I'm sorry if I made it sound like you have a choice. Because you don't.' Archer reached out his hand and grabbed hold of my arm. His long fingernails dug into my skin.

I heard a loud growl behind me. I quickly twisted my head round and saw that all the Shifters had shifted into their animal forms.

Archer suddenly didn't look so confident once a panther and a wolf were stood beside me baring their teeth. He quickly let go of my arm and took a step backwards. Then owl Amber flew straight at Archer's face, only veering at the last second, and scratched his cheek with her claws as she flew away.

'Ow, you stupid bird!' Archer said, as blood trickled down the side of his face. 'Fine, I give up. I'll leave. You continue to live your ordinary life with the pathetic Shifters and pitiful humans. But mark my words, you'll regret it.'

Archer turned to strut away with confidence, but then warthog Ed came bounding out of nowhere and nipped at his heels, causing him to have to sprint away with a shriek.

Once Archer was out of sight, the Shifters gradually began to shift back to their human forms.

'Mollie, are you okay?' Ava asked, running over to put a comforting arm round my shoulder.

'You must have been so scared,' Will said, looking

concerned.

'Surprisingly, no,' I said, looking round at my remarkable group of friends. 'How could I be scared with such a fierce team right behind me?'

Apparently, that was the cue for a massive group hug. Even Amber, Clara and Emma joined in. And in that moment, it felt like everything was going to be okay.

✧   ✧   ✧

MUM WAS STILL up when I got home. She was sat at the kitchen table wearing her dressing gown and cradling a cup of tea. Her eyes looked heavy and she tried to suppress a yawn.

'Hi, love.' Mum looked up and smiled.

'Hi, Mum. Is everything okay?'

'Come and sit down with me for a minute,' Mum said softly.

I perched on the edge of one of the wooden dining chairs. 'Am I in trouble?' I asked, my heart rate quickening.

'No, no, sweetie. I'm just worried about you. You haven't seemed like yourself recently. You would tell me if you were having difficulties, wouldn't you? I mean, if you were being bullied, or falling behind with your work? Or even boy trouble. I know I'm not good at talking about these things Mollie, but I'm always here and I'll always try to help.'

My eyes started to fill with tears. 'Thanks, Mum. I'm

sorry you've been worried about me. You're right, I haven't been myself lately, but I'm feeling much better now. Honestly.'

Mum's whole body seemed to visibly relax and she took a sip of her tea. 'You're sure you're okay?' she asked again, placing a hand gently on my arm.

'I'm sure, Mum. And I'm sorry I've been distant. Let's spend some time together. I'll book us a spa day. Just the two of us.'

'That sounds lovely,' Mum said with a tired smile. 'Now, I think I should go to bed.'

'Goodnight, Mum. Sleep tight.'

I went upstairs to bed as well but I couldn't sleep, there was too much I needed to process. It felt good to have started to make amends though. First with the Shifters and now with Mum. I hadn't tackled Rose yet. I knew I had hurt her the most of all and it was going to be difficult to gain her trust again. An apology seemed like the best place to start so I composed a text message;

Hi Rose. I don't know if you heard, but I'm back. I'm so sorry I left so suddenly. Things have been strange for me recently. But that's no excuse for being a bad friend. I'm going to tell you everything. Do you want to go to the County Fair together tomorrow? Come to mine before, around 5pm? Xxx

I switched off my bedside lamp, lay down and quickly fell into a deep dreamless sleep. I was woken briefly at one o'clock in the morning by my phone vibrating on my bedside table. It was a reply from Rose which simply read;

Fine.

Well, it was a start, I suppose.

CHAPTER 13

T HE COUNTY FAIR had become a yearly tradition for me and Rose, even though it was usually a bit of a disappointment. It generally rained, the rides were overpriced and we would spend a small fortune on funfair games, trying to win prizes we didn't even particularly want. It still had a nostalgic charm, though, and there would be people from college there, including the Shifters, so it could be fun. However, my main focus was Rose and making things up to her.

It wasn't long before Rose was due to arrive at my house and I sat on the edge of my bed trying to think how I was going to explain things to her. Where would I start? And would she even believe me? I didn't want to scare her or put her in danger but I knew our friendship wouldn't survive unless I could be completely honest with her.

At ten minutes past five there was a knock on the front door. I ran downstairs and pulled the door open. Rose was stood there in a brightly patterned, loose-fitting dress with a navy-blue cardigan, matching tights and black lace-up boots.

'You look nice,' I said.

'Thanks.'

'Is it cold out?'

'Yes, quite.'

It appeared I had some grovelling to do. 'Come on in. I'll get us a drink then we can go up to my room.'

Rose stepped inside, barely making eye contact with me. It felt like we were strangers.

When we got to my room Rose made herself comfortable on my bed and I sat on my desk chair, swinging from side to side and tapping my fingers on the arm of the chair.

After a couple of minutes silence Rose said in a low voice, 'I was so worried about you Mollie. Just disappearing like that with no explanation.'

'I know, I'm sorry. Something's happened to me Rose and I couldn't tell you before but I'm ready now.'

'Mollie, you know you can tell me anything. You're my best friend.'

Rose looked at me with her kind eyes full of concern. I knew my secret would be safe with her.

I started to try to explain. 'Okay … do you believe in aliens? Well no, not aliens, but the supernatural?' I wasn't explaining myself very well at all.

'Mollie, are you on drugs? We can get you help,' Rose said seriously.

'No!' I said with a nervous giggle. 'But it has sure felt

like it at times. Something strange happened to me, Rose, and I've been trying to deal with it, and process it, and embrace it, but it's been tough.'

Rose looked me straight in the eyes. 'Mollie. Just tell me. You're scaring me.'

'Okay, here it goes … I am a shapeshifter. I can change into whatever human form I like. Daisy, the new girl at college, that was actually me. I made her up because I thought I would have the perfect life. But now the Drifters are after me … they are shapeshifters but evil. I'll explain more about them later. The rest of the korfball team are shapeshifters too, but they can only shift into animals. Jamie is a panther, Matthew is a wolf, Amber is an owl—'

'Mollie,' Rose interrupted me and swiftly stood up from the bed. She looked tense and spoke to me slowly. 'Have you taken something?'

'No, of course not.'

'Then I think I need to go downstairs and find your mum. You're scaring me and I want to get you help. I didn't realise you were having a breakdown. I'm sorry I haven't been here for you.'

'No no no, don't tell my mum,' I said, jumping up from the chair. 'Honestly Rose, I know how mad it sounds, I didn't believe it at first either. But this is what I've been going through and I could really do with my best friend's support right now.'

Rose still didn't look convinced and I couldn't blame

her. I could see she was poised to make a dash for my bedroom door so she could go and find my mum. I needed to get her to believe me, and quick.

'I know what I can do, I'll just show you. You want to talk to my mum? I'll get her for you.'

I closed my eyes for a split second and shifted into Mum.

Rose blinked about a hundred times and looked around the room like she was expecting to find me hiding somewhere. She even bent down to have a quick look under the bed.

'It's me, Rose. I'm right here.' I really hope this works and doesn't make things worse.

Rose just continued to stare in disbelief.

'Hmm, who else should I do? How about Principal Golding?'

I shifted again.

'Good morning,' I said in a monotonous voice, 'and welcome to yet another assembly where I say absolutely nothing of use or interest and sound like I would rather be absolutely anywhere else on the planet.'

Rose wasn't finding me funny.

'Have you ever wondered what it would be like to have a twin?' I asked rhetorically as I shifted into Rose.

This time, Rose leapt up off the bed, tentatively walked over to me and studied my face and touched my hair (*her* hair) with a trembling hand.

'This isn't a trick?' she asked, her voice quiet and

trembling. 'You promise me you're telling the truth?'

'One hundred percent truth,' I said sincerely.

'Mollie, this is completely mad. How is this even possible?'

I had never seen Rose's eyes so wide. 'I wish I knew,' I said with a sigh. 'I'm still getting used to it myself.'

'I kind of wish you were just doing drugs; that would be easier to understand. I have so many questions. Like does it hurt? When you change shape, I mean?'

'Nope. It's a weird feeling, but it doesn't hurt.'

'And you can be anyone you want?'

'Anyone.'

'How have you been coping? I can't even imagine how you're meant to deal with something like this.'

'I've had the support of the korfball team, but I have missed talking to my best friend.' That was an understatement.

We hugged. Finally we could start getting back to normal.

'Er,' Rose said taking a step back, 'Do you think you could change back to yourself? You're freaking me out a bit.'

'Oh, of course. Sorry,' I said as I shifted back.

Rose lay down on my bed and stared at the ceiling. I lay down next to her.

'Wow,' she said.

'I know.'

'Yeah, but I meant, it's just like … wow.'

'Yeah, I know.'

We both laughed. I knew it was going to take a while for Rose to understand everything but I was so happy that she now knew and hadn't completely freaked out.

'Mollie, I've actually got something I need to tell you too.'

'Of course, what's up?'

Rose looked uncharacteristically nervous as she continued to stare at the ceiling. 'Well it's just that, umm, I like Jenny.'

'Rose, that's totally fine, don't be silly. I know we were inseparable at secondary school, but college is different. It's only natural we find new groups of friends.'

'No, no, you're not hearing me. I *really* like Jenny.'

'Ah.' The penny finally dropped.

'Well that's cool too, obviously. So are you two together?'

'I don't know, I don't really want to label anything yet. I always thought I liked guys. But with Jenny it's easy, and fun. So we're giving it a go, but taking things slowly.'

'Well that's very exciting, I'm happy for you.'

'You are?'

'Of course. Rose, if you can accept me being a shapeshifter, I think I can accept you liking a girl!'

Rose laughed. 'Well I guess when you put it that way maybe it's not such a big deal!'

'I'm really glad you told me.'

'So am I.' Rose instantly looked less tense, like a huge

weight had been lifted off her shoulders.

'Do you still want to go to the fair?' I asked. 'I completely understand if you've already had enough "excitement" this evening. We could stay in and watch a film instead?'

'No, no,' Rose said with a smile. 'I'm fine, and you deserve to go out and have some fun. Come on, grab your bag and let's go.'

The fair was around a twenty minute walk away through the local housing estates and it gave us a chance to catch up.

'So,' Rose said, 'tell me about life as Daisy? Weren't you dating Dan for a while?'

'Ugh, yeah, that was a huge mistake. I don't think he's a completely bad guy but I can't imagine him loving anyone else as much as he loves himself! By the way, watch out for the WAGs. They're not so nice either; they wanted me to throw a drink over you.'

'Oh, was that at the football match when Daisy ended up soaked? I felt so sorry for her, but I didn't realise you were trying to protect me. Thank you.'

'You don't need to thank me. It's one of the very few good things I've done recently.'

'Mollie, everyone has a tough time figuring out who they are, and you've been doing it under, well, some exceptional circumstances. Give yourself a break!'

I laughed and said, 'I guess you're right.' I knew Rose would know how to make me feel better.

As we neared the funfair I could hear the buzz of the crowd mixed with the hypnotising tunes of the fairground rides. The smell of candyfloss and fresh doughnuts filled the air. We entered the fair through the open mouth of a giant inflatable clown who had a bit of a sinister look about him.

'Where do you want to start? I'm up for anything except the Waltzers; they make me feel so sick!' Rose said.

'Yes, I know. I witnessed that first hand a few years ago, remember?!' I laughed.

It really was a sensory overload inside the fair and my eyes darted from the Waltzers to the coconut shy, from the dodgems to the carousel. The fair attracted people of all ages, from hyperactive toddlers to fun-loving grandparents.

'How about a drink and a sugar hit first?' I said, spotting the soft drink and candyfloss van.

'Perfect.'

We slipped our way through the crowd and Rose ordered for us both. 'Two large Cokes and two candyfloss sticks please.'

Whilst Rose was sorting out her change I tried to balance everything in my arms. I turned around and stepped forward before looking up properly and –

Splosh!

Drink everywhere. Actually my top had got off pretty lightly. The (previously) white T-shirt standing in front of me however …

'Argh! Cheers, clumsy! Look what you've done!'

It was Dan! And he was fuming. I just stood there staring at him, wondering if actual smoke would start coming out of his ears like it does in the cartoons.

Dan seemed to be on a date with yet another pretty girl who hissed at me, 'Well aren't you going to apologise?'

'Nope, actually I'm not,' I said simply as I walked away.

Rose came running after me.

'What was that about?' Rose asked with a giggle.

'That, Rose, is what you call karma.' And I had to admit, it felt good.

We walked around for a while, taking in all the sights and smells and sounds, when we came to the Hall of Mirrors.

'Do you fancy it?' Rose asked. It wasn't my favourite attraction but I knew Rose liked it so I said yes.

As we entered, there was a row of mirrors which distorted your reflection. In one I was very wide, then very thin, then I had a huge head and a tiny body. I looked straight ahead and kept walking. I had already seen my body go through enough changes recently. Rose was enjoying herself though, twirling around in front of all the different mirrors. We then came to the mirror maze. It was dimly lit and I immediately felt claustrophobic.

'This way!' Rose called. I tried to follow her but came

up against a solid mirror.

'Hey!' I cried out at my own reflection. 'Rose, are you there?'

'Yes, stick to the left I think!'

'I can't, it's a dead end.'

'Oh, okay. Maybe it was right then. Just keep walking …'

Her voice got quieter until I could no longer hear her over the eerie music they were pumping through the speakers. I hadn't realised quite how warm it was inside the maze. I looked at my flushed cheeks in the mirror right in front of me. I saw a dark figure out of the corner of my eye but when I turned to look it had gone.

'Rose?' I called out nervously.

I put my hands out in front of me, feeling where the gaps were as I couldn't rely on my vision which was being tricked.

Another flash of a tall, cloaked figure. Or was it just a trick of the light?

My fumbling hands started to move faster, desperate to find the route to freedom.

Pull yourself together, Mollie. It's only a funfair attraction.

One more step to the right and … Ah, fresh air! I blinked as my eyes adjusted to the light and looked around for Rose.

'Has my friend come out already?' I asked the man in the ticket booth. He just shrugged, completely uninterested. Helpful.

I texted Rose;

I finally made it out! Meet me by the ferris wheel? Xx

I ventured through the crowds towards the Ferris wheel and I noticed a couple of guys at the top leaning backwards and forwards to make their pod swing violently. I felt queasy just watching.

I looked around but still no sign of Rose. However, I did notice Matthew in the crowd. When he spotted me he waved with a big grin and came bounding over and gave me a hug.

'Hey, Mollie!'

'Uh, hi!' I said, a little taken aback by the public display of affection.

'Sorry, I'm a bit excitable; too much candyfloss. And I've just got off the Waltzers.' He put his hand on my shoulder to steady himself. 'Come on, let's go on the Ferris wheel together.'

'Actually, I can't right now. I'm just looking for Rose.'

Matthew clearly didn't hear me as he was already dragging me by the hand towards the end of the queue.

'Not many people know this but I'm a little afraid of heights,' I admitted.

'Don't worry, I'll be with you the whole time. Oh, and I got you this.' Matthew pulled a small cuddly bear out of the pocket in his hoodie. He held it out to me, looking very proud. 'I won it on the hook-a-duck.'

It was a sweet gift and it made me blush. Luckily Matthew didn't seem to notice, or he was too kind to point it out at least.

'I told Rose the truth this evening,' I said.

'Really? The whole truth?'

'The whole truth.'

'Wow, how did she take it?'

'Well, initially she thought I was on drugs or having a breakdown!'

'Can't blame her for thinking that to be fair.'

'Exactly. But then she was completely fine. And our secret is definitely safe with her, don't worry.'

When the next empty pod arrived Matthew got in first and I tentatively followed. The pod swung back and forth vigorously when I sat down. I grabbed hold of the bar to pull it tightly down over our laps just as Jamie popped up out of nowhere and slipped onto the seat beside me.

'Hey, guys. Mind if I join?' Jamie asked, albeit too late as we started our ascent.

I didn't look at Matthew's face to see his reaction but I could see his hands clenched around the metal bar to the point I was worried he might break it. Jamie wasn't holding on, as in his arms he was holding a huge cuddly toy dog. He caught me looking at it.

'I scored five out of five on the basketball shooting game,' he said proudly. 'Here, it's for you,' he continued, placing it on my lap.

Matthew's knuckles were now going white from how forcefully he was gripping the bar.

I felt queasy and wasn't sure if it was the swinging of the pod or the complete awkwardness of the situation.

'I felt uneasy in the hall of mirrors earlier,' I decided to confide in them both. 'Like maybe someone else was in there.'

'After everything you've been through, Mollie, it's not surprising you're a bit jumpy. I'm sure it was nothing,' Matthew said, trying to reassure me. However, I caught him giving Jamie a look which indicated he was, in fact, a little concerned.

Jamie said matter-of-factly, 'Look, I don't think the Drifters are going to just give up and leave you alone, but they would be pretty bold to make another move so quickly. My dad has nearly perfected the anti-shifting serum and he says when it is ready he and the Shifters committee will take down the Drifters. He said we just need to be patient.'

'And in the meantime I will protect you,' Matthew said.

'*We* will protect you,' Jamie added.

I began to feel a bit better and felt some of the tension leave my body, until I remembered where I was and all my muscles immediately tightened again.

The pod swayed in the wind as we reached the top and my stomach lurched as we started yet another descent. On my right, Matthew was looking away from me, his body still tense, whilst on my left Jamie seemed as relaxed as always and completely oblivious to the awkwardness. Please let this ride be over soon.

We finally slowed to a stop and I couldn't rip the safety bar up quickly enough. I waved a quick goodbye to Jamie and Matthew and managed to find Rose in the crowd.

'Hey!' she said, 'I'm sorry, I got a bit lost. There's so many people here, do you want to walk home now?'

'But you never want to leave the fair early! How about one more ride?'

'Okay, sure. How about the Waltzers?'

'Er, they make you feel sick, remember?'

'Yeah, of course. Not the Waltzers,' Rose said, shaking her head. 'I meant the dodgems.'

'Sounds good. I think they're over this way,' I said, setting off excitedly.

Rose was a little quiet and distant as we walked across the funfair to the dodgems. I spotted Dan and his new girlfriend in the queue just ahead of us. Great.

'He's still got the drink stain on his T-shirt!' I whispered to Rose who only responded with a half-smile.

'Rose, are you still mad at me? I can understand if you are, but I thought you had forgiven me? What else can I say or do?'

Rose's expression barely changed as she said, 'Mollie, everything's fine. I'm just tired and there are so many people here. I just want us to walk home together. We can take the short cut through the woods.'

Luckily it was our turn to get on the dodgems.

'Okay,' I said, 'we can go home right after I've shown you what an awesome driver I am!' I sprinted across the platform to get to the electric blue car with number twelve painted on the side, my lucky number. I clicked my seatbelt into place and beeped my horn.

Once the dodgems were full, the music and lights started up and the electric cables crackled above as the cars jolted to life.

It took me a couple of seconds to get used to the heavy steering. I drove up beside Rose. 'Heeeeey!' I shouted as I zoomed past. This was fun. I spotted the Shifters watching from the side. They all waved at me (apart from Amber) and I waved back. Due to my momentary lack of concentration my car veered slightly and I bumped into the side of Rose's car. She didn't look too impressed.

Dan was being a bit annoying in his car, bumping into everyone at high speed. He drove straight towards me so I veered left to try to get out of his way but he turned too and hit me on the side and my car jammed against the side of the track. Whilst I tried unsuccessfully to manoeuvre my car away from the edge, I watched Dan bump the back of Rose's car with force.

'Try that one more time, wise guy,' Rose shouted furiously.

'Okay,' Dan said, as he turned his car around then

drove straight towards her head on. Neither Dan nor Rose looked like they were going to pull out of the collision. I wanted to shout 'STOP!' but nothing came out of my mouth. They wouldn't have heard me anyway. They bumped against each other with a bang then flew off in opposite directions. Dan was finding the whole thing hilarious and continued off round the track in search of his next victim. Rose, however, was enraged. Her whole face and neck had turned bright red and she was shaking her fist angrily towards Dan and shouting something that I couldn't make out over the music and buzz of electricity. And that's when it happened. Rose's face flickered and she was no longer sweet Rose, she was an older man. Archer. It was only for a millisecond but the face was unmistakable.

I frantically looked around for the Shifters to try to signal to them but they had seen it too. 'Drifter!' they were all mouthing and pointing. I was still strapped in my car despite pulling furiously at my seatbelt, but the Shifters pushed their way to the front of the queue to try to get to Rose (Archer). The electricity suddenly cut out as the ride came to an end and the seatbelts were released. I watched helplessly as Rose (Archer) jumped out of the car and leapt over the railings into the crowd of the fair. I saw the Shifters rush off to try to catch him.

'Split up!' I heard Jamie yell out.

I was still sat in my car in shock. Then I felt a man's cold hand on my shoulder and I nearly jumped out of my skin. 'You need to get out, love. Your turn's over. Rejoin the queue if you want another go.' It was just the big bald man running the dodgems.

I couldn't form a sentence to reply so just scurried towards the exit. I tried in vain to look through the crowd and find where Archer and the Shifters had gone.

After what felt like a lifetime, I saw the Shifters walking back towards me. Their shoulders were hunched and they were dragging their feet. Ed in particular looked very out of breath.

'Did you catch him?' I asked, although I feared I already knew the answer.

'No,' Will replied. 'We lost him in the crowd and couldn't find him. Once we lost sight of him, we figured he could have shifted into anyone so we would never have found him.'

'Obviously we couldn't have shifted into animals in front of so many humans,' Jamie said, 'Otherwise there's no way he would have got away from me. Stupid, slimy Drifter.' He clenched his fists and I had never seen him look so angry.

'More importantly,' I said, my voice shaking, 'if that wasn't Rose then where is she?'

Everyone stared at me blankly. This wasn't helping my anxiety. Ava put a supportive arm round my shoulder.

'Wait a minute,' Matthew said. 'You told us you felt like there was someone else in the Hall of Mirrors with you and Rose earlier? What if Archer was there and he took Rose and then shifted into her place?'

Amber interjected, 'But why would he take Rose? The Drifters want Mollie, why not just take her?'

'That's true,' Matthew replied.

'It was pretty dark and disorienting in the Mirror Maze, maybe he just grabbed the wrong person?' I suggested. As soon as I had said it and saw the others nod in agreement, I felt a huge weight of guilt that Rose had been taken and this was all my fault. 'It should have been me,' I whispered, tears spilling from my eyes.

Jamie came over and lifted my chin with his fingers so I was looking up into his eyes. 'Listen. This is not your fault. And Rose will be fine. Like Amber said, it's you they want, so they'll likely use Rose as leverage, but they won't hurt her.'

'Okay, fine. Then how and when do we make the trade?' I asked.

'We are not trading you,' Matthew said.

'We're not?' Amber asked incredulously.

'No,' Jamie confirmed. 'Let's wait for the Drifters to get in touch, which they will, then we will form a plan. Mollie, can I stay at yours? I don't want you to be alone tonight.'

'Uh …' I wasn't quite sure what to say.

'Everyone can stay at mine!' Amber blurted out. 'We should all stick together.'

I couldn't quite work out if Amber was trying to be

nice and supportive or if she just didn't like the idea of Jamie staying at my house, but either way I didn't have the energy to argue.

'Perfect,' Jamie said. 'Let's get going.'

CHAPTER 14

I WALKED ALONE behind the rest of the group. I really wasn't in the mood for talking. I felt a huge weight on my shoulders as I dragged my tired feet along the pavement.

I heard Emma whisper to Amber, 'What is your mum going to say about you having boys to stay over?'

'It'll be fine,' Amber hissed back. 'She had a work thing today and she's staying at a hotel overnight. She'll never know.'

Ava dropped back to walk beside me. 'She'll be okay, you know,' she said softly.

'I really hope so,' I said, looking up at the stars and making a silent wish.

We eventually reached Amber's house and walked up her long driveway. It was pitch black now but the house was all lit up and looked like a mini castle.

'Wow,' I heard Will and Ed gawp in unison.

'Amber, you didn't tell us you were rich!' Will joked.

'I'm not,' said Amber, embarrassed, as she opened the grand front door and disabled the alarm.

'Yeah right!' Ed said, looking round at all the expensive artwork and vases decorating the hallway.

'Make yourselves comfortable in the lounge,' Amber said. 'I'll go and find bedding for everyone.' She climbed a couple of stairs before turning around and adding, 'Just *please*, don't touch anything.'

I sunk down into one of the soft leather sofas with a sigh. I felt like I was in a dream. Actually, a nightmare.

Matthew sat down next to me. 'Stupid question,' he said, 'but how are you doing?'

'I feel so guilty,' I admitted, staring down at my hands. I was wearing a silver bracelet with a star pendant that Rose had given me for my sixteenth birthday. I rubbed the pendant between my finger and thumb as though it would bring me luck.

'No one could have predicted this happening,' Matthew said. 'You did nothing wrong.'

Nothing he said was going to reassure me. I just needed to know that Rose was safe.

I felt a vibration in my pocket. It was a text message. From Rose's number.

'Hey!' I shouted out to get everyone's attention. The whole room fell silent as everyone turned and saw me staring at the phone in my trembling hand. 'It's from the Drifters,' I clarified. I was so anxious I could barely talk.

'Do you want me to read it?' Matthew asked softly.

'No, it's okay.' I needed to be strong. For Rose. 'Mollie. It appears we have something of value to you. And you have something incredibly valuable to us. Join us, work with us, fulfil your destiny and we will set your useless human friend free. Fifty-one Cliveden Avenue, London, tomorrow at 9 p.m. we will make the trade. Come alone. Her freedom for yours. Yours faithfully, Mr Silverman.'

When I looked up from reading the message I could see the veins in Jamie's neck bulging as he paced in front of the marble fireplace.

In comparison, I felt calm for the first time since Rose had been taken. I knew where she was and I knew how to get her back. *Her freedom for yours.* I would do whatever it took.

Jamie's voice cut through my train of thought. 'I need to tell my dad. He and the committee will know what to do. I'll just give them the address and they can go down there and sort it out.'

'Jamie, you can't!' I cried, 'Mr Silverman said to come alone. I'm not letting anyone else get involved and I'm not letting anyone else get hurt. This is my fight.'

'No, this is *our* fight,' Will said emphatically.

'Yeah,' everyone else joined in, even Amber.

'Okay, hear me out. I have an idea,' I said. 'Jamie, if you could get hold of your dad's anti-shifting serum for me then all I need to do is get all the Drifters to drink it.'

'And how will you do that?' Clara asked. 'You can't exactly waltz into their lair and expect them to accept a random drink from you.'

'No, you're right, they wouldn't accept a drink from me, but they would accept a drink from Mr Silverman,' I said. 'So we lure him away from the group somehow, then I take his place.'

'This sounds far too dangerous,' Matthew chimed in.

'I agree,' Jamie said, 'You don't have enough experience shifting under such extreme conditions.'

'And what is the alternative?' I asked.

Silence.

'Precisely,' I said defiantly as I crossed my arms. No one was going to change my mind.

'But we need a proper plan,' Ed said in a rare moment of seriousness.

'I'll do it,' Amber said. 'I'll fly down there now and get an aerial view of their address so we can see what we're working with and make a proper plan.'

'Why don't you wait until the morning, Amber,' Emma said stifling a yawn. 'It's been a long day.'

'It's fine, 'Amber replied. 'Besides, my eyesight is better at night.'

Before anyone could argue any further, Amber shifted in the middle of the lounge into her majestic owl form and Ava opened a window so she could fly out into the dark night.

'Thank you,' I called after her, although I wasn't sure how good an owl's hearing was and whether she would have heard me.

After Amber had left on her information-gathering

mission, the rest of us started to lay out blankets and pillows on the floor so we could try to get some sleep. However, the thought of being able to switch off and sleep seemed unlikely.

The mood in the room was very subdued and no one was saying much except for the odd small talk.

'Reckon there's any biscuits in the kitchen?' Ed asked hopefully.

'Nope. Amber's mum doesn't allow any refined sugar in the house,' Clara replied.

'That's a shame, I reckon Ed is at least fifty percent refined sugar after the amount of candyfloss he ate tonight!' Will joked.

I couldn't help but smile for the first time since Rose went missing. Lovely, innocent Rose. I wished so desperately that Amber would come back with some good news.

I sat back down on the sofa under a blanket between Matthew and Ava. They didn't need to say anything for me to feel their support. My eyelids felt so heavy. I tried to fight it but I slipped into a deep dreamless sleep. I had no idea how long I was asleep for before I was suddenly awoken to the sound of flapping owl wings. I jerked my head up and realised I had fallen asleep on Matthew's shoulder. I quickly checked the sleeve of his T-shirt for any drool marks.

Amber shifted back into her human form and everyone just stared at her expectantly.

'Okay,' she said eventually, 'I found the house. Well, it's more of a mansion. Rose is being kept in an outbuilding at the bottom of the garden and—'

'Is she alright?' I couldn't help interrupting, I needed to know.

'Yes, she's fine,' Amber said. 'There were no Drifters within sight so I managed to shift back for a minute and talk to her. She said they hadn't hurt her, they just locked her up in the outbuilding and someone comes to check on her every hour. She said Mr Silverman had been to see her and told her he would personally bring her up to the main house an hour before the trade. There was a big hefty padlock on the door. I tried to peck at it but there's no way we're getting in there without the key.'

'That's all really useful information, Amber. Anything else?' Jamie asked.

'Well,' Amber said, 'Rose did ask me to promise her that Mollie wouldn't be put in any danger if we try to rescue her.'

'That's so like Rose,' I said, 'but it's not her call to make. I'll do whatever it takes to get her home safely.'

'Okay,' Matthew said, clearly wise enough to know not to argue with me, 'so what's the plan?'

'Right, so let's think,' I said. 'We know Mr Silverman will be at the outbuilding at 8 p.m. to take Rose back to the house. So we lie in wait. Then we force Mr Silverman to release Rose and trap him instead. Then, I shift into him and return to the house with the anti-shifting serum to use on all the other Drifters.'

'Wait,' Will said. 'But if we manage to rescue Rose, why do you need to risk going inside to take on the Drifters?'

'Because,' I said, 'we need to disarm their powers for a while. Slow them down. You saw how quickly this has all escalated. If we just rescue Rose they will come straight after us, and who knows what they will do next time.'

Silence and sideways glances.

'She's right,' Jamie eventually conceded. 'Mollie, I'll get you the anti-shifting serum. By the time my dad notices it's missing it will be too late for him to stop us. But I cannot stress enough how risky this is.' It was rare for Jamie to sound so genuinely worried.

'I understand fully,' I said.

'I feel like there are a lot of holes in this plan,' Matthew said, looking around the room for some agreement.

'It's not a perfect plan,' Jamie said, 'but right now it's all we've got. And I have full faith in our team. Let's get some sleep now. We'll leave for London tomorrow at 7 p.m. from the college sports field. It'll be getting dark by then so we can run there.'

'Or fly,' Amber added.

'Sorry, or *fly*,' Jamie said with a smile.

Everyone started to settle down into their makeshift beds. Somehow I had been lucky enough to get the big leather sofa.

'Goodnight, Shifters,' Ed called out.

'Goodnight,' everyone echoed back. I was so drained it didn't take me long to fall back into a deep sleep.

When I opened my eyes it was still quite dark. The air in the room smelt musty and smoky to the point it was almost suffocating. I got up and took a couple of steps forward. Ouch! I bumped into a cool, hard surface. It was a mirror. I turned and stepped to my right. Another mirror. And another on my left. I was surrounded. Trapped. 'Help!' I tried to shout out but no sounds came out of my mouth. I started to panic. I closed my eyes so I could concentrate without staring at all my reflections. When I opened them again I was back in Amber's living room.

Phew. Just a nightmare. Still, it took a minute for my breathing to settle and my panic to subside.

I heard a car driving up the gravel driveway and a car door slam shut. This woke most of the others, including Amber, who jumped up off the floor. She still looked perfect even first thing in the morning.

'Huh? Is that Mum? She's not due back until later!' Amber rushed to the window and opened the curtain slightly so she could peer out. 'Aah! Quick everyone, help me tidy all the bedding away and then get out! ... Quickly!'

'Amber, we're never going to have time to tidy up and get out. Your mum is literally right outside,' Emma said, clearly still groggy with sleep and rubbing her eyes.

'I'm going to be grounded for life!' Amber wailed.

'Three things you must never bring into this house Amber,' she continued, impersonating her mother. 'Number one: refined sugar. Number two: drugs. Number three: boys.'

Wow, that is quite the list.

I had an idea. And before I had time to talk myself out of it, I rushed out of the living room, down the hallway and opened the front door. And came face to face with Amber's mum who was just about to put her key in the door.

'Oh!' Amber's mum said in surprise. 'Principal Golding, what are you doing in my house? Has Amber done something wrong?' She seemed uncharacteristically flustered.

'Good morning, Mrs Walton. I'm so sorry for the unannounced visit. Amber was kind enough to let me in and offer me a cup of tea. She's not in any trouble, don't worry.'

'Okay. So, then, may I ask what are you doing here?'

That was a good question.

'Well,' I said, becoming a little flustered myself, 'I am visiting a few select students today. And why? Well, because, well it's because I am hand delivering awards. Good news, Amber has won an award!'

Nailed it.

'Oh, fabulous! What for?'

'Music student of the year.' I knew music was Amber's passion and she played first violin in the college orchestra.

'Oh, right, that's great,' Amber's mum said without a hint of enthusiasm.

'She really is very gifted,' I said.

'Don't get me wrong, I'm pleased she has a hobby. But it's hardly a career, is it? Like being a lawyer, for example.'

She looked Principal Golding straight in the eyes and I felt compelled to stand up for Amber. 'Actually, there are many fantastic career opportunities in music, especially with a talent such as Amber's. I tend to find students flourish and accomplish most in the subjects they enjoy. To force someone down a path they do not wish to go down would be very unwise.'

I would never have dared say any of that to Amber's mum as myself, but being Principal Golding gave me the confidence and authority.

'Well, Principal Golding,' Amber's mum said, barely hiding her irritation, 'thank you so much for coming. I suppose you have a very busy day ahead of you so please don't let me keep you.'

'Thank you, Mrs Walton,' I said as I stepped past her out onto the doorstep. The front door was quickly slammed behind me. I only hoped I had stalled her enough to give the others time to sneak out of the house. I waited on the doorstep for a few seconds and didn't hear any screaming so assumed it must have worked. I felt rather pleased with myself. It was a shame I had a feeling the rest of the day was not going to be quite so straight forward.

CHAPTER 15

I SPENT THE day practising my shifting in my room. I shifted into everyone I could think of and tried to get every detail exactly right because that was what I needed to do if I was going to fool the Drifters. They were the experts in human shifting and I was sure they would see straight through me if I so much as hesitated.

Knock knock

I quickly shifted back to myself and pretended to be doing my coursework as Mum opened the door. My head was spinning from all the shifting.

'Are you still working, love? That college does seem to be working you hard!'

'Yep, it's just a particularly tricky assignment this week,' I lied. The truth was I had been falling behind with my coursework, but it wasn't like I could ask the teachers for an extension; *'Sorry I haven't had time for homework this week, I was a little busy trying to rescue my friend from an evil group of shapeshifters.'*

'Well I brought you more snacks,' Mum said presenting me with a plate of biscuits.

'Thanks Mum.' I didn't tell her that I felt too sick to eat.

'You're welcome,' Mum said as she headed back downstairs.

Right, back to practising my shifting. I shifted into all the other Shifters in turn then threw in a few of my favourite celebrities for extra practice.

Knock knock

Mum poked her head round the door again.

'Mum, I don't need any more snacks!' I snapped. I appreciated her trying to look after me but I really needed to concentrate.

'I know, love. It's just there's a young man at the door for you. He said his name is Jamie, I think he's been here once before. Should I let him in?'

'Oh, yes please,' I said, suddenly a little flustered.

Mum left to go back downstairs but then poked her head round the door again and said with a grin, 'I must say, he's rather dishy!'

Argh, I wished the ground would swallow me up! And hoped with all my might that Jamie hadn't heard that.

I heard heavy footsteps on the stairs then Jamie pushed open my bedroom door.

'Soo,' he said with a smirk, 'your mum thinks I'm "dishy"!'

I laughed. 'Don't let it go to your head!'

Jamie's mood quickly changed from jovial to very

serious as he sat down on my bed. He reached into the pocket of his leather jacket and pulled out a glass pipette bottle. I instantly knew what it was. The bottle was so plain looking, yet the liquid it held was so incredibly powerful. Jamie cradled the bottle delicately in his hands and stared at it.

'I stole it,' he said finally. 'I feel awful not telling Dad what's going on, but I know it's the best chance we have of getting Rose back safely and taking down the Drifters.'

'I can do this,' I said placing a hand on his arm. 'I've been practising. I'm ready.'

'I admire your confidence Mollie, I really do. But tonight you will be under a lot of stress and you'll really have to hold your nerve. But if anything starts to go south I'll be right outside ready to pounce.'

'I don't doubt that for a second.'

'Right, I should give you this then.' He handed me the glass bottle of anti-shifting serum, although for a second he seemed reluctant to actually let go of it. 'It only needs a drop per Drifter. Like I said, it should force them to shift back to their original forms and make them weak. But Dad was still tweaking the formula so we won't know exactly how effective it will be. So once they have drank it you will need to get out of the house ASAP.' He looked me in the eyes. 'Promise me.'

'Stop worrying so much!' I wasn't used to Jamie being so serious.

'I can't help it. I'm meant to be your mentor and I

can't help but feel I let you down.'

'No. If anything I've let myself down, the way I've acted at times. I haven't understood what's really important in life. I know now.'

'I've never met anyone like you, Mollie.'

'I'm going to take that as a compliment?'

Jamie smiled and got up to leave, not offering any further explanation of his comment. Mysterious and frustrating as always. 'Get some rest now and I'll see you later,' he said as he stole one of my biscuits on his way out of my room. 'Goodbye, Mrs Thomas!' I heard him call out cheekily through a mouthful of biscuit before he shut the front door.

So many thoughts were racing round in my head. But one thought was particularly intrusive – what if I didn't make it out of the house? What if I was forced to join the Drifters? I was willing to sacrifice myself to save Rose, but I also knew it would destroy Mum if I didn't come home. I decided to write her a letter. I tore a page out of my notebook, found a biro and started to scrawl;

Mum,

If you are reading this then please know that I didn't choose to leave you, I had to. I'm so sorry I can't be there for you like you have always been for me, but please know that I have left for a very good reason. I have always admired your strength and resilience and I hope that some of it has been in-

stilled in me. Please don't be sad and please don't look for me. I will come home if and when I can.

I love you. Always.
Mollie xxx

A tear fell from my cheek onto the paper. I folded it in half and left it on my pillow so Mum would find it if I didn't come home.

A few long hours later I left for the college sports field. I knew I would be there early but I didn't want to be late and I couldn't handle being sat at home anymore with only my thoughts for company. There was a chill in the air already and I knew it would only get colder, so I had wrapped myself up in a thick coat and long woolly scarf.

When I got to the field it was eerily quiet. Then I saw a shadow approaching. An instantly recognisable, friendly shadow. Matthew.

'You're early,' Matthew said as he gave me a hug.

'I couldn't sit at home any longer.'

'Same,' Matthew said. I looked at Matthew's face under the glow of the field's floodlights and could see the tension written all over his face.

'Are you okay?' I asked.

'To be honest, I wish you weren't in this situation. And I wish I could do more.'

'Do more?' I exclaimed. 'Matthew, you have been my rock every step of this journey and I don't know what I would do without you. So don't ever feel like you haven't done enough.'

'That's nice of you to say. It's not going to stop me worrying about you tonight though.'

I didn't know what to say to reassure him. I certainly couldn't promise him that everything would definitely be okay.

'Matthew, if I don't make it out—'

'Don't say that; it's not even an option.'

'No, listen, but if I don't, then I want you to do something for me.' Matthew leaned towards me, listening intently. 'I want you to have my calculator. It's in my locker. You're going to need it to get through the rest of the year without me!'

'You're an idiot!' Matthew laughed. At least I had made him smile and relax a little.

The rest of the Shifters gradually started to arrive and I noticed everyone was unusually quiet. Ed even refrained from making his usual jokes. We were all shivering in the cold so we huddled together and went over the plan. Shift and make our way into London. Lie in wait for Mr Silverman to make an appearance. Free Rose and trap Mr Silverman. Then I enter the house with the anti-shifting serum as Mr Silverman. The details of the plan from that point forward were a little less precise as we didn't know what the situation would be inside the house. I would have to improvise. Think on my feet. Not something I was particularly good at to be honest, but no need for the others to know that.

'Mollie, are you listening?' Jamie asked. Oops, I had zoned out for a second. 'Can you promise me that if you have any concerns when you enter the house and you don't think you can administer the serum then you will just get out of there?'

'I promise,' I said. I knew better than to try to argue with Jamie.

I saw Matthew raise his eyebrows and I knew that he knew that I would be following through with the plan to take down the Drifters, no matter what.

'Let's get going then!' Will said enthusiastically, trying to lift the mood.

In the blink of an eye I was no longer surrounded by humans but by magnificent animals. I would never get used to the extraordinary sight. I kind of wished I could shift into an animal, not least because then the Drifters wouldn't be after me. I started to ponder which animal I would like to be when panther Jamie nudged the back of my knees. I climbed on his back and wrapped my arms round his neck. I remembered from last time just how tightly I had to hold on.

Owl Amber flapped her wings and flew off and the others followed. Fast. The wind rushed past my ears yet I could still hear the sound of panther Jamie panting. I could also hear the occasional grunt from warthog Ed. It was oddly reassuring.

After around an hour, owl Amber came to rest in a

tall leafy tree and I realised we had reached our destination. I carefully climbed off Jamie's back. My legs felt like jelly. Panther Jamie clawed at the bottom of a fence panel to create a hole for us to get through. I tried to dodge the mud that was flying into the air. My body tightened with each scratching sound, terrified that the Drifters would hear. Everyone then shifted back to their human forms so they would be able to fit through the hole in the fence.

'I guess it's showtime,' Ed said.

'Are you ready?' Matthew asked seriously, placing a hand on my shoulder.

'As I'll ever be,' I replied, forcing a wry smile.

'Follow me,' Amber whispered, kneeling down to crawl through the fence.

Once inside, we crawled to the left following the fence around the perimeter of the garden, under the cover of darkness. I could see a dim light being emitted from the outbuilding straight ahead. My heart started pounding, knowing Rose was caged inside. But we couldn't see her. Not yet. Instead we stopped a few metres away and stood up, pressing ourselves against the fence. Silent and still.

I realised I had been holding my breath the entire time. In. Out. In. Out. You can do this Mollie.

Half an hour of unbearably tense waiting later, a shadow advanced towards us from the house. Tall and slim. Walking with confidence. Wearing a long flowing coat. As he neared I could make out a few more features from the light of the outbuilding. He had silver hair, just like his name. Pale, smooth skin which almost glistened. In short, he was very handsome. It was a shame he was also very evil.

I took a deep breath and boldly stepped out of the shadows and stood in front of the wooden outbuilding.

'Mollie, what a pleasure,' Mr Silverman said, not at all flustered by my unexpected arrival. 'We would have welcomed you through the front door you know. We even have champagne ready.' He studied me with his bright blue eyes and it made my skin crawl. 'I'm Mr—'

'I know who you are,' I said bluntly.

'You're angry,' Mr Silverman said with a sigh. 'And I understand, Mollie. Really, I do. It was never our intention to involve a human in this. That was a mistake, and one Archer will pay for. But in our defence, if you had just joined us when we asked nicely …'

'If you ask someone then that implies they have a choice,' I argued.

'Ah yes, that's true. And you really don't have a choice. You were born to be a Drifter. To rise above the humans and the dirty animal Shifters.'

I could hear panther Jamie growl behind me in response to that comment but Mr Silverman didn't seem to notice.

'It's not too late for you to do the right thing,' I said.

'The right thing?' Mr Silverman laughed. 'Did my parents do the right thing when they threw me out of the house after I started shapeshifting because they thought I was cursed? Did the government do the right thing telling shapeshifters that we would never be accepted?'

'I'm sorry for what you've gone through,' I said sincerely, 'but you can't use it to justify your behaviour.'

'I've actually had enough of the lecture, and now it's time that we—'

'Actually, it's time you let my friend go. Right now,' I said, my confidence growing.

'I think you are confused,' Mr Silverman hissed. 'I don't take orders from anyone. Especially not from a little girl.'

At that moment, panther Jamie leapt from the shadows and pounced on Mr Silverman. He placed his big paws either side of Mr Silverman's chest and pushed him roughly to the ground with a thud.

'Dirty Shifter!' Mr Silverman spat in panther Jamie's face, which made him bare his full set of canines. Mr Silverman's eyes widened as he struggled to hide his fear. He seemed to be weighing up his options. Realising he had very few, he gently nodded his head. Panther Jamie stepped off him, one paw at a time, and Mr Silverman gingerly got to his feet. He reached into his pocket and pulled out a key but then turned and looked at the house.

'Don't even think about shouting or running; panthers have super quick reaction times. And super sharp teeth,' I warned.

For some reason, probably fuelled by his narcissism, Mr Silverman fancied his chances against a panther. He quickly turned and started sprinting back towards the house. Panther Jamie and wolf Matthew set off in quick pursuit. It was actually Matthew who reached Mr Silverman first. Matthew managed to grab the back of Mr Silverman's coat between his teeth. This sent Mr Silverman crashing face first to the ground and Matthew dragged him back down the garden through the mud.

Once Matthew let him go, Mr Silverman scrambled to his feet. He looked exhausted as he eventually relented and went to unlock the padlock on the outhouse. 'You won't get away with this,' he muttered.

All the other Shifters, except Ava, were in their animal forms and closed in around Mr Silverman so he couldn't get away.

The padlock clicked open and fell to the floor. Rose pushed open the wooden door and ran straight over to me for a hug.

Ava stepped forwards. 'Now get in,' she told Mr Silverman.

'No way. I did as you wanted, I let your friend go, now I'm going back to the house.'

'We're not stupid,' Ava said. 'We know you would just come straight after us. Mollie is going to take down your army of followers. Well, actually, you are …'

Ava gestured in my direction as I had already shifted into Mr Silverman. I didn't know how well I had shifted but his shocked and angry reaction suggested I had done alright. 'You won't get away with this,' he said again. 'My loyal followers will know you're an imposter.'

Wolf Matthew strode forwards towards Mr Silverman until he was so terrified he actually shut himself in the outbuilding. Ava picked up the padlock from the floor and clicked it shut. Then she flung the key over the fence.

Mr Silverman just stood glaring at me (himself) through the dusty window of the outbuilding.

'Mollie, what are you doing?' Rose whispered.

'There's just something I need to do. I won't be long. Stay here with the Shifters, they will look after you.'

Ava ran over to me. 'You've got this,' she said with a reassuring smile.

'If I'm not out in twenty minutes you get Rose and the other Shifters to safety, okay?' I said.

Ava started to protest but I had already started to walk towards the house. My heart was pounding in Mr Silverman's chest. Despite the cool weather I was starting to sweat in his long leather coat.

The house was imposing from a distance but even more impressive close up. I found a side entrance. I reached out a trembling hand and tried the silver door knob. It turned. I stepped inside into what appeared to be a utility room. Lots of cupboards and spotlessly clean work surfaces. There was no one around but I could hear a hum of activity coming from further inside the house. I stepped through another door into a very grand kitchen. Everything from the lighting to the appliances oozed opulence. On the huge marble-topped island sat a silver tray of filled champagne glasses. Perfect.

I glanced around then pulled the anti-shifting serum bottle from my pocket. My hands were shaking so much I almost dropped the delicate glass bottle. There were thirteen glasses. At least that gave me an idea how many Drifters I was dealing with. I used the pipette to put a single drop into each champagne glass except for the one closest to me which I would keep for myself.

Deep breath. I carefully picked up the tray and followed the sound of the voices. It lead me to the lounge. Or probably one of many lounges. When I entered everyone suddenly stopped talking. All twelve Drifters stared at me and nodded their heads in respect. I quickly surveyed my surroundings. A couple of plush dark-blue velvet sofas either side of a roaring fireplace. A crystal chandelier hung elegantly from the ceiling. The ceiling was high and had a fancy mural painted on it. As for the Drifters themselves, they were all stunningly beautiful. Most of them were men, but there were also a few women scattered around the room. Both men and women were very well dressed and dripping in expensive jewellery.

I needed to stop gawping. What should I say? I cleared my throat. 'My devoted Drifters, I thought it was time we had a toast,' I said, holding out the tray of champagne. I hoped they didn't notice the tray shaking slightly.

Archer came siding over to me and said quietly, 'Umm, Mr Silverman, I thought we were saving the celebrations until after we have made the trade?'

'Why are you questioning me? It's never too early to celebrate. Now take a glass of champagne.'

'You can't be handing out the drinks, Mr Silverman. Here, let me do it.' Archer tried to take the tray from me, but I gripped on tightly. Archer was staring at me and kept pulling at the tray. We engaged in a mini tug-of-war until eventually I had to let go and Archer walked off to hand out the champagne. I tried to follow the tray with my eyes to keep track of where the unpoisoned glass was but Archer turned his back and I lost sight of it.

Another Drifter appeared beside me. He wore a dark-blue suit with silver cufflinks. Both his hair and his eyes were a rich dark brown. He spoke in a serious, hushed voice. 'Mr Silverman, I hope I am not overstepping but I just wonder whether we have really thought this through. Should we really be forcing the young girl to join us? She might be more trouble than she's worth. And now an innocent human is involved. I wonder if we should just set her free.'

I took a moment to imagine how Mr Silverman would have reacted to these surprising comments.

'An innocent human?' I said angrily. 'There is no such thing! And as for Mollie, we haven't found a new Drifter for years, we need her youth and her abilities. She should fulfil her destiny. The door's right there if you want out.' I wasn't actually entirely sure where the front door was, so hoped I was pointing in vaguely the right direction. I stared intensely at the Drifter until he broke eye contact.

'No, no Mr Silverman,' the Drifter said. 'So sorry, I didn't mean to offend,' he grovelled, bowing his head and slipping away behind me towards the door to the kitchen.

I couldn't help but feel he was lucky I wasn't the real Mr Silverman after those traitorous comments.

Archer sauntered back over to me carrying the final two glasses of champagne, one for me and one for him. I took the one closest to me. I had no idea at this point which one didn't contain the serum anyway. If luck was on my side then, by some miracle, I was holding it in my hand. If not, well then my evening had just got a whole lot worse.

Everyone was looking at me expectantly again. I raised my glass and studied the tiny bubbles rising to the surface, wondering if they contained the anti-shifting serum.

'I would like to make a toast to the Drifters and to an exciting new chapter on our path to world domination. Cheers!' I said.

'Cheers!' everyone responded. But no one put their glasses to their lips. Had they realised I was an imposter? My stomach leapt into my throat and my mouth went very dry.

'Cheers!' I said again whilst raising my glass even higher. They were still staring. Then I realised they were respectfully waiting for me to take a sip first. I put the glass to my lips and took a sip of the expensive champagne. There was no other way I could get the Drifters to drink theirs without raising suspicions. The tiny bubbles exploded on my tongue. My heart pounded as I looked around the room waiting for something to happen. I had no idea how long it was going to take.

I didn't have to wait long until one by one the Drifters gasped and fell to their knees. Their faces flickered between their stunning shifted forms and their natural, older selves. They struggled to stand as their bodies changed and became weaker.

'Mr Silverman!' Archer called out to me from the floor. 'What's happening?' Archer no longer looked like a stunning young man, but a very ordinary looking, frail older man. I almost felt sorry for him. Almost.

My job was done, I needed to get out of the house. I turned and took a couple of steps towards the kitchen before my knees buckled and I fell to the ground. My head was spinning and my eyes were blurry. I could feel my body forcibly shifting back to its natural self despite me desperately trying to hold onto Mr Silverman's form. It was the strangest sensation and all I could do was drag myself along the floor. I could vaguely hear one of the Drifter women panicking from the other side of the lounge, shouting, 'What's happening to you all? Help, someone help!' She must have had the glass without the serum and I knew I had to escape before she pulled herself together and figured out what had happened.

There was a Drifter by the door to the kitchen. He looked even weaker than me so I hoped I would be able to crawl right past him. The Drifters were being affected more by the serum because they had been persistently shifted from their natural selves for much longer than I had.

As I dragged myself past the Drifter, I managed to hold my head up to look him in the face. I expected to hate him. But to my surprise, he had kind eyes. Mousey-brown thinning hair, wrinkles and a prominent nose. The face looked older than the last time I had seen it, yet it was instantly recognisable.

'Dad?' I gasped.

'Mollie,' he said. He took a deep and laboured breath. The effort of talking was too much.

'You're a Drifter?' I asked, stunned.

'No, well yes, but I'm a mole. I only infiltrated them to try to take them down. All I ever wanted was to protect you.'

'But you left me! You left Mum.'

'Oh Mollie,' he said, tears filling his eyes. 'I didn't want to. But I knew there was a good chance you would have human shifting abilities like me, and I knew the best way to protect you from the Drifters was from the inside.'

Dad could barely catch his breath.

'Dad, I'm so sorry. I didn't mean to hurt you. It's just an anti-shifting serum, you should recover and get your strength back eventually. Follow me, crawl towards the back door.' I started to crawl away, expecting Dad to follow.

'Mollie, I can't. I need to maintain my cover; I can influence them from the inside. I'm trying to turn the others against Mr Silverman and get them to see this isn't how they have to live their lives.'

'But Dad …' Now my eyes were filling with tears. 'I miss you so much.'

'Me too Mollie, more than you'll ever know, but you need to go. Now. Look after your mum for me.'

'But—'

'Now!'

Luckily we were hidden by the huge sofa but I knew if I talked to him any longer someone would see us and his cover would be blown. But I didn't want to lose him. Not again.

'I'm so proud of you,' Dad said. 'Now go!'

I struggled to see through my tears as I dragged myself through the doorway into the kitchen. The tiled floor was cold and slippery. I made my way past the kitchen island and into the utility room. I felt woozy and completely drained of energy. I used my very last ounce of strength to reach up for the doorknob to open the way back to the garden and the Shifters.

And that's when everything went black.

CHAPTER 16

B LINKING, I SLOWLY opened my eyes. It took them a
while to focus. It was still quite dark and I had no
idea what time it was. This wasn't my room. But I
recognised it. I was lying in a comfy double bed under a
brightly coloured duvet. I rolled over onto my other side.
Ouch, I felt bruised. Lying next to me was Rose. Thank
goodness. She started to stir.

'Hey,' I said.

'Hey you. How are you feeling?'

'Okay, I suppose. A bit tired and achy. What happened? I don't remember making it out of the house.'

'Well, once you had been in there for twenty minutes,
Jamie and Matthew went up to investigate. They found
you passed out just inside the doorway so they dragged
you out down the garden and carried you home.'

'And you're okay?' I asked. 'The Drifters didn't hurt
you?'

'Yes, I'm absolutely fine. Thanks to you.'

I heard a loud snore come from the end of the bed
and looked at Rose in shock and confusion.

'Oh yeah,' she said, 'Matthew insisted on staying overnight. He wouldn't leave your side. He said he wanted to make sure you're okay.'

'Oh, that's sweet.'

'Very,' Rose said with a grin.

'Mollie?' Matthew called out. I peered over the end of the bed and saw Matthew sleeping on the floor wrapped up in a duvet. His hair was sticking out at all angles and he was rubbing his eyes.

'Good morning,' I said. 'What are you doing down there?!'

'You were in a right state, Mollie. I'd never seen someone look so weak. But it looks like you've made a quick recovery.'

'I hear you saved me. Again. Thank you.'

'You did all the hard work. You managed to get the anti-shifting serum into the majority of the Drifters. It should take them a while to recover. And even though Mr Silverman was spared he can't do anything without his followers. And besides, he'll need to find his way out of the outbuilding first!'

It was strange to hear Matthew talking about last night. It felt like a dream. I was so glad the plan had worked and everyone was safe, but something was playing on my mind. 'I need to tell you guys something,' I said seriously. Matthew and Rose looked at me, concerned. 'Something happened in the house. When the Drifters were forced to shift back, I recognised one of them. It was my dad.'

Matthew and Rose's jaws dropped open.

'Your dad is a Drifter?' Matthew whispered. 'Why? How?'

'We didn't have long to talk. He said he infiltrated them to take them down from the inside and to protect me.' I paused and a rush of emotion flooded over me thinking back to the brief but special conversation. 'And he said he was proud of me.' Rose leaned over and gave me a hug.

'Wow,' Matthew said. 'How do you feel?'

'I'm not sure yet. I think it's going to take a while to sink in.'

'Of course,' Rose said.

'This is huge news, Mollie. Let's talk more about it later, but I'm afraid right now I need to get going,' Matthew said, climbing out of his duvet cocoon and up off the floor. 'I need to see if I can sneak back into my room before my parents notice I was gone!'

'Good luck,' I said. 'And thank you again.'

I lay my fuzzy head back down on my pillow. It felt good to rest.

'Go back to sleep if you want to,' Rose said.

'I would love to, but I need to get back too. Mum will be so worried I didn't go home last night.' And what if she finds the letter I wrote?

'All taken care of. I texted her from your phone to tell her you were staying over at mine. I said we were working on a college project and lost track of time.'

I sighed with relief. 'What would I do without you?'

'Who knows? Now, get some rest then in the afternoon we'll go dress shopping in town for the college Christmas party tonight.'

The Christmas party. I had completely forgotten about it given everything going on.

'Oh, I'm not sure I'm up to it,' I said.

'It's not up for discussion! We can't miss it, even if we don't stay late. I love Christmas; the fairy lights, the tinsel, the cheesy music. And besides, you deserve some fun.'

'Fun sounds good. Let me sleep on it.'

'Alright, sleep well.' Rose tucked me in gently before she headed downstairs.

When I woke up again a few hours later I felt much more alert and my muscles were no longer aching. Rose popped her head round the door.

'I made you pancakes,' she said, presenting me with a plate stacked high with American style pancakes topped with berries and cream.

'That's amazing, thank you. You didn't have to.'

'I wanted to get your strength up so we could go into town and then to the party?' Rose asked hopefully. I sat up in bed and took the mouth-watering plate from her.

'How could I say no?' I said.

I felt much better once I had eaten, showered and dressed. We wrapped up warm and walked into town.

Tanglewood town centre wasn't so bad. It had some cobbled streets, a few clothes shops and plenty of cafes and restaurants. No expense had been spared on the Christmas decorations this year and right in the middle of town was the biggest Christmas tree I had ever seen. The smell of roasted chestnuts wafted through the air and we found ourselves wandering towards one of the carts.

'Two bags, please,' I said. Rose went to pull out her purse but I stopped her. 'I'll pay for them,' I said.

'Hey look,' Rose said excitedly, gesturing to our left. 'Reindeer!'

The local children's hospice always raised money by driving a sleigh round the town. Santa would sit in the sleigh and wave at everyone whilst his elves would walk alongside jingling their collection boxes. This year it seemed they had gone all out with reindeer too.

Rose has always loved animals so we ventured nearer. On closer inspection they were in fact ponies wearing fake antlers.

'I'll give him ten minutes, then we'll have to go without him,' we heard one of the women say.

'But we can't have a sleigh without a Santa!' another woman shrieked.

Then a third woman came stomping over, waving her phone. 'I just got hold of his wife. He's hungover. Can't get out of bed! Argh, these rent-a-Santas are so unreliable!'

Rose and I looked at each other, bemused.

'This means we won't be able to fund the children's pantomime visit this year,' one of the women said sadly.

Rose looked like she'd had an idea and she stared at me for a few seconds, eyebrows raised, until I caught on.

'Oh no, I don't think I'm up for more shifting at the moment.'

'But it's for the children!' Rose said.

She was right. This was a perfect way to use my abilities for something good. 'Okay, wait here a minute.'

I scuttled away to a quiet alleyway, imagined a plump, jolly, bearded Santa and closed my eyes for a second. I walked back towards Rose and caught my reflection in a shop mirror. Not bad! I particularly liked my red velvet coat with white fur trim and thick black belt.

I strolled over towards the women and their empty sleigh. They didn't notice me at first so I thought I would introduce myself with a loud, 'Ho ho ho!'

'Are you the rent-a-Santa?' one of the women said abruptly. 'You can't just turn up late and hungover.'

'No no no, I'm the real Santa. I've come from the North Pole. And I don't drink.' I flashed them my best Santa smile.

'Well you do look like the real Santa and you don't smell of booze, so you'll have to do!' one of the women declared.

'I have brought my head elf with me,' I said nodding

towards Rose, 'but she forgot her outfit. Can she ride in the sleigh with me?'

'Of course. We have a spare elf hat she can wear.'

'Perfect.' This was surreal.

Rose looked like an excited child on Christmas morning as she climbed onto the sleigh. She wore a green bobble hat with large pointy elf ears sticking out of the sides. We set off through the town, waving at everyone from babies to grandparents. The collection boxes seemed to be getting heavier with everyone's kind donations.

'This is amazing!' Rose exclaimed.

It really was. 'We might have to make this a yearly tradition!' I whispered to Rose.

An hour later we had finished our loop of the town. My arm was cramping from all the waving and my beard was starting to itch.

'Thanks so much Santa,' one of the women said. 'We'll have to count up but it seems like one of our most successful years of fundraising yet.'

'Ho ho ho, Merry Christmas, and thank you for everything you do for the children,' I said as Rose and I walked away with a spring in our step.

'We had better head home,' I said.

'But we never got a chance to go dress shopping!'

'It doesn't matter, we did something more important. We can wear something old.'

'You're right. When did you get so wise Mollie Thomas?'

I just laughed and stroked my long white beard.

CHAPTER 17

I ARRIVED BACK at home late afternoon, having shifted back to myself in a quiet part of town. I found Mum in the kitchen preparing dinner. I ran over and gave her a big hug.

'Hi, love. Did you have a good night with Rose?'

'Yes thanks, Mum.'

'You look tired,' she said, concerned.

'It was just a long night of studying. Also, I was just, uh, wondering, could I go to the college Christmas party tonight?'

'Yes, you can go.'

I was a little shocked. 'No interrogation of where, when, who and curfew times?!' I joked.

Mum put her potato peeler down with a sigh. 'I've been talking to my friends at book club. They agree I need to give you more space. Let you grow up a little. So although I really, really want to ask you all those questions, I am trying to give you some freedom.'

'Aww, thanks Mum. I don't mind that you're a little overprotective, there are worse things in the world. And I think I am growing up, but I can't imagine a time when I won't still need my mum!'

We hugged again and Mum squeezed me so tight I could barely breathe.

'Is Rose coming round to get ready for the party?' Mum asked. 'It would be lovely to see her and there's plenty enough dinner for her too.'

'No, not tonight. I was actually wondering whether you could help me get ready?'

'Really?' Mum asked, a beaming smile spreading across her face. 'That sounds good. Let me just get this shepherd's pie in the oven.'

I went upstairs for a shower. It felt so good to wash away all the events of the past couple of days. I slipped into a dressing gown and sat at my desk to do my make-up. It was a relief to see my own face looking back at me in the mirror, not Daisy's or Mr Silverman's or even Santa's!

Mum popped her head round the door, 'Do you want me to do your hair for you?'

'Yes please,' I said handing her my hairbrush and hairdryer. Once my hair was dry, Mum started clipping some sections back.

'It's been a good few years since I've done your hair,' Mum said. 'When you were little you made me style it in two plaits tied with red ribbons every day. You refused to go to school until it was done!'

I laughed. 'I don't remember that.'

'Wait a second,' Mum said as she popped to her bedroom. She came back clutching a small leather box in her hands. 'I was going through some old boxes from the loft and I found this necklace.' Mum carefully opened the box to reveal a silver chain with a sapphire pendant. 'Your father gave it to me on our wedding day. It brings back too many painful memories for me, but I thought you might like it.'

The sapphire was dazzling blue and it twinkled in the light. 'It's beautiful Mum. Are you sure?'

'I'm sure,' she said fastening it delicately round my neck.

I wish I could tell her more about Dad. Especially that he didn't leave us by choice.

'Mum,' I said, unsure exactly what to say, 'I think Dad was a good man. I think he must have left for a good reason. I don't think he was trying to hurt us or didn't love us anymore.'

Mum was silent, tears forming in her eyes. 'Mollie, when I have my rational head on and I'm not feeling too angry or sad about what happened, I believe that too. And besides, I can't hate him. He gave me the greatest gift of all.'

'This necklace?'

'No, *you*, silly!'

Mum gave my hair one last brush then left me to get dressed. I slipped into a little black dress and did a twirl in the mirror. It was an old dress but my new necklace really set it off. And it was nice feeling close to Dad.

It was a dark and chilly evening so Mum kindly gave me a lift to the party. 'Have fun!' she said as I climbed out of the car at the college entrance. I was very impressed she had resisted giving me her usual speech on the way to the party: no alcohol, no drugs, no boys, home by midnight … I knew it off by heart anyway.

I walked up the path to the college doors as I had done so many times before. But this time it felt like a weight had been lifted. There were fairy lights lining the path and more adorning the front of the college. It actually looked very tasteful and Christmassy, except maybe for the huge inflatable snowman.

Once inside I could hear classic Christmas songs echoing from the great hall. I walked into what looked like a Santa's grotto. Red and green balloons, tinsel, a huge Christmas tree, even fake snow being pumped into the air. I was impressed. Rose was right, this was just what I needed.

'Mollie!' Ava came running over and gave me a big hug. 'You look great. The Shifters are all over here. Come and join us.'

'Merry Christmas!' the Shifters all shouted as I joined the group. Everyone had scrubbed up well and Ed was even wearing a red velvet bow tie. As I looked around the circle I realised how different we all were, yet all united by something very special and extraordinary.

'How are you doing Mollie?' Will asked, 'We were so

worried about you after you drank the anti-shifting serum.'

'Ah, you don't need to worry about me,' I said with a smile.

'Yes, we do,' Amber said, putting her arm round my shoulder, 'because we're a team and teammates look out for each other.'

Well, that was unexpected. But nice. Or maybe she was drunk?

'I just want to thank you all for your support,' I said. 'It's been a strange few months and I couldn't have got through it without you all, but I hope now we can get back to normal. Or as normal as possible, anyway!'

'Cheers to that!' Ed said. 'Now, I heard there were mince pies around somewhere … I'm going to go and sniff them out. I'll be back in a minute.'

'Mince pies? Wait for me!' Will said, chasing after him.

Amber turned to face me and held out her hand. I shook it, confused. 'I don't think I ever really welcomed you to the team,' she said. 'I'll admit it, I was a little jealous. Okay, a lot jealous. Until you joined, I was the newest member and everyone was impressed with my ability to fly. Then when you came along … Well, anyway, now you've shown everyone just how badass you are, and I like it. The world needs more strong women like you, Mollie.'

'That's really kind of you, Amber. No one has ever

described me as strong and badass before! The truth is, I've always been jealous of you. You always seem so confident and know exactly what you want.'

'No one's life is as perfect as it seems, Mollie, trust me. Although Mum has been a little more supportive of my musical ambitions recently. I think you may have had something to do with it … thank you.'

'Amber, if you ever need someone to talk to …'

'Woah, hold on a second. We're teammates, not friends, not just yet!' Amber said with a smile.

I knew it might take a long time to fully gain Amber's trust but I was willing to persevere and at least we had made a start in repairing our relationship.

I chatted with the Shifters for a while longer, then found Rose for a quick dance. The great hall was filling up and becoming a bit hot and stuffy, so I left Rose with Jenny and snuck away to get some fresh air. I had to squeeze past Dan, who was stood in the doorway with his arms around yet another pretty girl. I found an empty bench outside and sat down. My feet were grateful for the rest, I wasn't used to wearing heels.

As much as I wanted to switch off and just have fun, I found my mind wandering to the Drifters. How long would it take them to regain their strength? Would they continue to come after me? Had Dad managed to keep his cover? Worrying about it wasn't going to help and my fingers were beginning to go numb, so I decided to go back inside. However, before I had prised myself off the bench, I saw Jamie walking right towards me. He sat down beside me on the bench but didn't say a word. He seemed nervous. Or maybe he was just shaking with the cold.

'So,' Jamie said eventually, 'my dad was super mad about me stealing his anti-shifting serum. He grounded me, so I had to sneak out this evening. So when he finds out I'll be double grounded! I think he was secretly impressed with what we managed to do though. Maybe he'll involve us more in the Shifters committee plans from now on. Now that you've shown how amazing you are.'

'Oh, I don't know about that,' I said, blushing. I had managed to learn to control my shifting when I was embarrassed but my cheeks still gave me away every time.

'You *are* amazing Mollie. The things you've done in such a short space of time. Who knows what you'll achieve next year.' He looked at me with his intense, mesmerising stare. 'The things *we* can achieve.' Jamie closed his eyes and leaned in for a kiss and I instinctively leaned backwards. He looked surprised and even I felt surprised that I had reacted in that way.

'Jamie,' I said, trying to sort through my feelings, a million thoughts running through my mind. 'You're a great guy, really great, and you're gorgeous, and any girl would be lucky to have you. But I just don't think we're meant to be together. I think I was in awe of you, and I think you like me because of my special ability. But there needs to be more to a relationship than that. We both deserve better than that.'

I tried to look him in the eyes but his head had dropped towards the floor. 'I get what you're saying,' he said softly.

'This might not be the right time to be saying this,' I said tentatively, 'but what about Amber? She really likes you and you seem to have great chemistry.'

'I do like her,' Jamie said, 'but she can be so mean to people.'

'I get it,' I said, 'I really do. But sit down and talk to her. Really talk. You might find it's all just a front and there's a reason she's the way she is. I think you two would be great together if you could just break down those walls.'

'You know what, Mollie,' Jamie said, finally looking me in the eyes again and grinning. 'You might just be right.'

Jamie gave me a hug with his muscular arms and just as I was beginning to question whether I was being mad turning him down, he walked back into the party. If someone had told me three months ago that one day I would be turning down the hottest guy in college I wouldn't have believed them for a second.

I took a long, deep breath in. When I exhaled my breath created a misty cloud in the air. As it cleared I saw a familiar figure walking towards me.

'Hi geek,' Matthew said, sitting down next to me.

'How are you feeling?'

'Much better, thanks. I'm glad I came. It's really put me in a festive mood after a difficult couple of days.'

'That's an understatement! Have you thought any more about your dad?'

'Constantly,' I admitted. 'I hate to think of him trapped with the awful Drifters. Having to take orders from Mr Silverman. You know, whilst I was shifted as Mr Silverman my dad tried to convince him to let me and Rose go. He risked the wrath of the Drifters to try to save me.'

'Putting others before himself. He sounds like somebody else I know,' Matthew said, putting his arm round my shoulders which had started to shiver in the cold. I put my head down on his shoulder. I always felt safe with Matthew.

'I can't believe I've only known you a few months and you're already one of my best friends,' I said.

'Oh,' Matthew pulled away and sat with hunched shoulders.

'What?' I asked.

'Nothing, it doesn't matter.'

'I didn't mean to upset you,' I said.

'Okay, so here's the truth,' Matthew said, his voice shaking a little. 'I was going to ask you out on a date. Like a proper date. But you totally just friend-zoned me! I like you, Mollie. I think you're incredible.'

'Matthew, I like you too. A lot.'

'But …'

'But … I think I need some time by myself. I'm only just figuring out who I am and who I want to be. I don't want to rush into anything with you and ruin our friendship.' I knew it sounded so clichéd but if there was anything I had learned over the past few months it was that it's always best to be honest. I just hoped that Matthew would understand.

'I respect what you're saying,' Matthew said. 'It doesn't mean I like it, but I respect it!'

'Listen, I'm not saying no, I'm just saying not yet. Can you give me some time to figure things out?'

'Always.'

'Still friends?' I asked.

'I'll get those friendship bracelets ordered!' Matthew joked.

I gave him a playful shove. 'Do you want to go back inside before we both freeze?' I asked, to which Matthew nodded.

'Mollie!' Rose greeted me at the door. 'I've been looking for you everywhere. Come and dance with me?' She looked so excited and her festive bauble earrings glistened in the light of the disco ball hanging above us.

I looked up at Matthew apologetically. 'Go,' he said. 'Have fun.' I gave him a big hug and it took all my strength to pull away.

'Merry Christmas Matthew,' I said as Rose took my hand and dragged me away to the centre of the dance floor.

'What was all that about?' Rose shouted over the music.

'I'll tell you later. The rest of the night is about me and you.'

We danced non-stop until the lights came on and the music stopped. My dancing was as terrible as always, but for the first time ever I couldn't have cared less what anyone thought of me.

CHAPTER 18

THE REST OF the term was spent counting down the days to the Christmas holidays. If the threat of mock exams in the New Year hadn't been looming over me, then I think I would have switched off completely. I was drained and looking forward to a quiet Christmas with Mum; eating chocolate until we felt sick and re-watching our favourite festive films for the millionth time.

On Christmas Eve I went into town with Rose to do some last-minute shopping. The shops were always a bit hectic, but we planned to wind down at Rose's house with a film afterwards.

'Do you like this?' Rose asked, holding up a silver charm bracelet.

'Yeah, it's pretty. But I'm not sure if it's really your mum's style?'

'It's not for Mum, it's for Jenny. Is that a really stupid idea though? We're not even officially in a relationship? What if she hates it? What if she thinks I'm moving too fast?'

I placed a hand on Rose's shoulder to calm her down.

'Rose. If you chose it for her, she will love it. Don't overthink it.' I guided her towards the tills before she could change her mind.

After paying, Rose skipped back over to me, looking very pleased with her purchase which had been gift wrapped and tied with a red bow.

'Are you ready to head back to mine?' Rose asked. 'I made mince pies yesterday. I'll be honest, they don't look too pretty, but they taste great.'

'Actually, do you mind if I bail? I feel bad not keeping up our tradition, but it's been such a crazy few months and I think it might be nice to just chill out at home with Mum tonight.'

'Of course, that makes perfect sense. Let's walk home.'

Before parting ways we hugged and exchanged Christmas wishes. 'Try to stay out of trouble!' Rose called out as she walked away. I smiled. That was something I definitely planned on doing.

I opened the front door and pulled off my winter boots. The house was nice and warm and I could smell mulled wine coming from the kitchen and hear the television playing in the lounge.

'Right, what film do you want to watch first?' I asked, as I slipped off my coat and stepped into the lounge.

There was a strange man in the lounge. Sitting on our sofa. Cosied up next to mum. He had thinning grey hair and wore a hideous Christmas jumper.

Mum jumped up from the sofa and all the colour drained from her face. 'Mollie, what are you doing here? I thought you were spending the evening with Rose?'

'Who's this?' I asked, purposely ignoring her questions.

'Hello love, I'm Jeremy. It's so nice to meet you, Mollie. How was your little shopping trip?'

He didn't even attempt to get up from the sofa. He seemed very comfortable, so had clearly been in the house before.

'How long has this been going on for?' I asked Mum. 'When were you going to tell me? Please tell me he's not spending Christmas with us?'

Mum looked horrified. I didn't care.

'Perhaps I should leave,' Jeremy said.

'No, please stay,' Mum pleaded.

'It's fine,' Jeremy said, his tone sickly-sweet. 'I have daughters myself. I would never want to make anyone feel uncomfortable.'

'Thanks, Jeremy,' Mum said. 'I'll call you later. Let me just parcel up some Christmas cake for you to take home with you.'

Jeremy smiled at Mum. But as soon as she had left the room his whole expression changed.

'Listen, you little brat,' he whispered. 'I'm not trying to be your new step-daddy, I just want to date your mum, so stay out of it, okay?'

I was stunned, but managed to whisper back, 'Good,

because I already have a Dad,' before Mum came back into the room.

'I really am sorry, Jeremy,' Mum said.

'It's no problem at all.' His voice was all sickly-sweet again. 'Mollie and I have come to an understanding.'

We all moved into the hallway. I have never wanted to punch someone in the face so badly.

'Merry Christmas,' Jeremy said, whilst planting a sloppy kiss on Mum's cheek. I slammed the door behind him then stormed up to my room. Mum didn't come up to check on me, which meant she must have been really mad with me. Or too busy talking on the phone with her horrible boyfriend.

UNSURPRISINGLY, THE REST of the Christmas holidays were slightly awkward. I was so happy to restart college in January and even felt ready to throw myself in to exam preparation. But I was most excited to let off some steam with the Shifters at korfball practice.

'Mollie!' Matthew was the first to greet me as I entered the sports hall.

'Hi Matthew,' I said whilst giving him a slightly awkward hug. We had texted a bit over the holidays, but I think Matthew had been trying to give me space following our conversation at the Christmas party. I really hoped we could get back to how we were. 'How was your break?' I asked.

'Great, thanks. My little sister still loves Christmas so Mum goes all out with decorations and traditions. How about you?'

'Yeah, same,' I lied.

'Welcome back, everyone,' Jamie said. 'I hope you all had a good break. Just to update you, my dad hasn't heard of any more activity from the Drifters, so it seems they are still weakened. Thanks to Mollie.'

I received a small round of applause. 'It wasn't just me,' I protested.

'So, whilst things are quiet on the Drifters front, why don't we concentrate on korfball?' Jamie said, spinning a ball on his finger. 'We've got a lot of matches this term.'

And so we played korfball. Everyone was relaxed and happy, even Amber. It felt strange, but nice. Normality was nice.

Amber came over to me during a water break. 'So, how was your holiday?' she asked.

'Oh, it was fine, thank you,' I replied, automatically. 'Actually … it was a bit rubbish. I found out on Christmas Eve that Mum has a secret boyfriend. And he's disgusting.' It felt odd telling Amber when I hadn't even told Matthew. But if anyone would understand, I felt it would be her.

'Oh wow, that is rubbish,' Amber said. 'Do you want help to drive him away? I'm sure together we could come up with a plan.'

'That's really … sweet … of you Amber. I'll give him

a bit longer, but I'll let you know if I need your help. Thanks.'

Amber shrugged and walked away to talk to Jamie. The way they put their arms around each other suggested things had progressed over the holidays.

To finish the session we played a shooting competition where the aim was to stay in the game as long as possible. We played three times and Jamie won every time, despite Matthew's best efforts. I came somewhere in the middle, but poor Ed lost all three times.

'Too many mince pies over the holidays, Ed?' Will called out as we started to put away the equipment. Knowing Will's sense of humour and his relationship with Ed, he was clearly joking, but it was maybe a bit of a mean thing to say infront of everyone.

Ed looked down at his shiny new trainers and said quietly, 'I'll think I'll stay behind and practice my shooting.'

'Okay mate,' Jamie said. 'Just remember to put the post away in the cupboard when you're done.'

The rest of us walked home together, the group gradually getting smaller as people split off in the direction of their houses. I was beginning to get tired of the cold, dark evenings and looked forward to the warmth of summer.

The next day the Shifters gathered for lunch in the canteen between classes. We didn't do it every day, but taking down the Drifters together had definitely brought us closer.

'My legs are so sore after yesterday's session,' Clara moaned.

'Same here, I could barely get out of bed this morning,' Emma said.

Jamie clearly didn't feel very sympathetic as I caught him rolling his eyes.

'Has anyone seen Ed today?' Will asked through a mouthful of questionable-looking beef pie. Everyone shook their heads. 'He wasn't in our economics class this morning and he never skips classes.'

'Have you messaged him?' Ava asked. 'Maybe he just slept through his alarm.'

'Yeah, I've tried his phone but he's ignoring me. I guess I'll just try again later.'

'I'm sure he's fine, stop worrying,' Jamie said whilst giving Will a pat on the back.

By the next morning, it was clear that Ed wasn't fine. The local newspapers, the radio and internet articles all had the same headline:

Tanglewood teenager Edward Mumble MISSING.

CHAPTER 19

I T TURNED OUT Ed's parents had been worried the moment he didn't come home after korfball training. They phoned the police but he wasn't officially classed as missing until twenty-four hours had passed.

The police came into college to question students and staff. It seemed to put the whole college on edge. This kind of thing didn't usually happen in Tanglewood.

The Shifters arranged to meet in a corner of the playing field so we could talk in private. We huddled together and kept looking over our shoulders to make sure no one, especially the police, were within earshot.

'What did the police ask you?' Matthew questioned the group.

'They asked me when I had last seen him and how he seemed,' Emma responded.

'And what did you say?' Jamie asked.

'The truth. That he had been at korfball training but had stayed behind after we all left and that he had seemed fine,' Emma said with a shrug of her shoulders.

'No one's questioned me yet,' Will said. He looked

pale. 'Should I tell them that I teased Ed and that's why he stayed behind to practice his shooting, so really this is all my fault?'

'No,' Ava said firmly, putting an arm round his shoulder. 'You don't say any of that because it's not true. This is not your fault.'

'I think we all know whose fault this is,' Jamie said through clenched teeth.

'But I thought the Drifters were still too weak?' I said.

'Clearly not,' Amber said. Even she looked uncharacteristically shaken up by everything going on.

'Then we need to go and rescue him,' I said. I started to feel sick, wondering if this was about me again and the Drifters were using Ed as leverage. Perhaps the Shifters would never be safe as long as I was around.

'Mollie,' Matthew said, giving me a nudge. 'You zoned out for a bit there, what are you thinking?'

'Oh, nothing,' I replied.

'Let's not rush into anything,' Jamie said. 'We don't really have any idea what's going on. I'll speak with my dad tonight. And in the meantime, just answer the police's questions. It's not their fault they're looking in all the wrong places.'

'Ed's parents are both human. They'll have no idea what's really going on either,' Will said, shaking his head sadly.

'Right, chin up Shifters,' Matthew said, making eye contact with each of us in turn. 'We're going to work this out.'

'Agreed,' Ava said. 'Let's just get through the rest of the day. You never know, Ed might just turn up and tell us it was all a big prank.'

We all smiled. Although it was unlikely to happen, it was a nice thought.

'Shh, I can see the police,' Amber hissed. We all dispersed, trying not to look too guilty.

I knew I wouldn't be able to concentrate anyway, so I skipped my afternoon chemistry lesson and went into town with Rose. We wandered around aimlessly before finding a fast food restaurant.

'Double cheese and bacon burger with extra-large fries please,' I said as we reached the counter. Rose gave me a sideways glace. 'What?' I said, 'Stress makes me hungry.'

'No judgement here. I'll have the same please.'

We found a quiet table in the corner where we wouldn't be overheard. My burger didn't taste as good as I'd hoped it would.

'So what's the Shifter's plan?' Rose asked.

'To sit and wait,' I said through a mouthful of over-salted chips.

Rose's face didn't hide her surprise. 'But when I was kidnapped you came up with a plan to rescue me straight away?'

'I guess things are more complicated this time. Jamie said we have to wait.'

'And why is Jamie still in charge? You know you're the most powerful Shifter, don't you?'

Rose had been making it clear to me recently that she wasn't Jamie's biggest fan. 'Jamie played a big part in saving you, you know Rose.'

'That doesn't mean I have to like him,' she said with a shrug of her shoulders. 'Whilst we're on the topic of boys … when are you going to let Matthew take you out on a date?'

She had, however, turned in to Matthew's biggest cheerleader. I stuffed the rest of my burger in my mouth and indicated to Rose that, unfortunately, I was unable to respond to her question.

We walked home slowly; the food had made us lethargic. I pushed open the front door and hung up my coat. I really wanted to creep straight to bed, but since I was trying to repair my relationship with Mum, I thought I should probably poke my head in the lounge and say goodnight.

'Hi Mollie,' five different voices chorused. Damn, I forgot it was book club night.

The usual suspects were there, wine glasses in hand. But there was also a new face. A rather pretty face that I recognised but couldn't quite place.

Mum must have caught me staring at her. 'Sorry Mollie, this is Candace. It's her first meeting.'

'And I'm learning a lot,' Candace said, raising her wine glass with an irritating giggle.

Suddenly I twigged. She was a Drifter. The one Drifter that didn't drink the anti-shifting serum. And now she was in my house.

I wanted to run and hide in my bedroom, but I didn't want to leave Mum in a room with her. I could feel myself breaking in to a sweat. I needed time to think.

'I'm just going to get a drink,' I said whilst backing out of the room.

'Oh, I'll join you,' Candace said, standing up before I could say no.

I backed up to the kitchen drawer where we kept the sharpest knives. 'Why are you here?' I asked.

'Why do you think?'

'Because you took Ed, and now you want to use him as leverage to get to me.'

'If you think that, then you know nothing.'

'You tell me what's going on then.' I wasn't really in the mood for games when she was standing in my kitchen uninvited.

'We saw on the news that one of your group had been taken, but it wasn't us. One of the Drifters has been taken too. And since most of us are still weakened, Mr Silverman would like to call a short truce.'

'I don't trust a word that comes out of Mr Silverman's dirty mouth.'

'Mollie, we really need to work together on this. You're going to want to hear our plan. I suggest you get the rest of your little group on board.'

'I suggest you get the hell out of my house.'

Candace started to move towards me threateningly, but just as my hand went searching for the handle of the knife drawer, Mum burst into the kitchen.

'Did you find everything you need?' Mum asked with a smile.

'Yes, thank you,' Candace replied. 'And actually, I'm afraid I really must be going, I've got an awful headache. Must be the wine. Thank you so much for your hospitality.'

'Of course,' Mum said. 'And we look forward to seeing you again at the next meeting.'

'I wouldn't miss it for the world,' Candace said whilst looking me straight in the eyes.

I slammed the door behind her the second she stepped out of the house. I had definitely had enough of unwelcome visitors.

CHAPTER 20

THE NEXT DAY at college I went to speak to Jamie. I had wanted to talk to him alone, but he insisted that whatever I had to say, I could say infront of Amber too. So I told them both everything that had happened with Candace.

'Thank goodness you're okay,' Amber said, her eyes wide with shock.

Jamie had remained silent throughout my story and seemed deep in thought.

'We're not going to work together with the Drifters,' I said. 'Right?'

Jamie looked away and didn't answer me.

'This Candace woman was clearly lying,' Amber said, siding with me. 'I'm happy to fly down there, to see if they've got Ed locked in the outbuilding like they did with Rose.'

'No,' Jamie said. 'Let me run this new information past Dad and see what he says.'

'Since when are you so cautious?' I asked. I tried, and failed, to hide the annoyance in my voice.

'Since we almost lost you, Mollie,' Jamie replied, his voice a little shaky.

Jamie went to reach out his hand towards mine but then quickly stopped himself. Apparently though, it was a moment too late, as Amber got up to leave abruptly. 'I feel like there's a moment happening here,' she said frostily, 'that I'm clearly not a part of.'

'No, Amber, don't go,' I said as Amber flicked her long hair over her shoulder and marched away. I really didn't mean to come between her and Jamie.

Jamie shook his head. 'Don't worry, I'll talk to her later. I can tell you're not happy either. Why don't we ring my dad now, I'll put him on speakerphone and we can come up with a plan together.'

My pulse quickened. 'Oh, I don't know, I'm sure he'd rather just speak with you.' I didn't want to admit to Jamie how intimidating I found his dad. But he had already started to make the call.

'Hi Dad. Listen, I've got—'

'Son, I'm in a meeting. Is this important?'

'Yes, Mollie needs to tell you something about the Drifters.'

'Okay, I've got five minutes. Tell me.'

No pressure, then. But I told him, and he seemed to be listening intently.

'But I don't know how useful any of this is,' I said at the end. 'Because obviously we can't work with the Drifters.'

There was a pause on the other end of the phone and a small sigh.

'Mollie. Jamie. I'm afraid I don't see what other choice we have. We have no other leads. If the Drifters say they have a plan, then I think we need to at least hear them out. We can go to their mansion tonight, that way we'll have the element of surprise. Plus they're the ones that want us involved and they are still weakened, so we'll be entering from a position of strength.'

'Okay, Mr Peterson. If that's what you think's best, then good luck and be careful.' I was hardly in a position to argue with him and tell him I thought it was a terrible idea.

'Call me Paul. Actually, you should come with us, Mollie.' Jamie and I looked at one another, both as shocked as the other.

'Me? Really?'

'Of course. You've already shown your strength and courage. Both things we could use. I'll meet you both after college at six o'clock.'

'We could skip classes and leave earlier?' Jamie suggested.

'Your education remains the number one priority, Jamie. No matter what.'

Jamie scowled. 'Okay, Dad, six o'clock then.' Jamie hung up the phone, then continued to stare at it. 'Let's not tell the others what we've planned. I don't want to worry them.'

I didn't have the energy to argue. I was too busy worrying about what we were getting ourselves in to.

At five minutes to six, Jamie and I waited on the sports field for his dad to appear. I hopped from foot to foot to try to keep warm. Meanwhile, Jamie seemed unusually tense.

'So, how are things going with Amber?' I asked, trying to break the awkward silence.

Jamie just raised his eyebrows at me.

'Sorry,' I said, shaking my head. 'You're right, it's none of my business.'

'No, it's fine, it's not that,' Jamie said. 'And things are good. It's just … feelings don't just disappear, if you see what I mean.'

I froze. I had no idea how to respond to that. But luckily I didn't have to. A large eagle swooped down from the sky and landed on the branch of a nearby tree.

'That's Dad,' Jamie said, as if I hadn't already figured that out for myself.

'Are you okay to ride with me again?' Jamie asked.

I nodded, seeing as I didn't really have a choice. Jamie took a step away from me then shifted into his panther form. I could barely make him out anymore against the dark sky. I reached my hand down to locate his back and then gently climbed on.

Panther Jamie ran as quickly and silently as always and the cold air hit my face, taking my breath away. I looked up at the sky occasionally and could just about make out Paul keeping watch from above.

We re-grouped close to the Drifter's mansion.

'Okay,' Paul said. 'I'll take the lead. You two stay behind me and keep your eyes and ears open.'

Jamie and I just nodded. My heart was beginning to race seeing the front door of the mansion. I had tried my best to suppress the thought of getting to see Dad again, but as we walked up the path and Paul knocked on the door, I thought I might throw up in one of the plant pots.

Jamie squeezed my hand but kept looking straight ahead as Candace pulled open the grand front door. She didn't say anything, just stepped aside to let us in. I still hated her for weaselling her way into my house. But she looked much weaker and paler than she had done yesterday. What had happened to her?

She led us to the lounge which I was already familiar with. The layout had changed though. My eyes darted round the room, trying to take everything in. The sofas were placed round the edge of the room and draped across them were the poisoned Drifters, still weak and in their original forms. I couldn't see Dad though.

In the centre of the room was a long wooden table, covered with a midnight blue tablecloth, with tall candles standing at either end. In the middle of the table sat Mr Silverman. I could barely bring myself to look at him as he stood up.

'Ah, I've been expecting you,' he said.

'We didn't tell you we were coming,' Paul said bluntly. He stood his ground and if he was at all nervous, he certainly wasn't showing it.

'You didn't have to. Not when I can see the future.'

Paul laughed. 'Yeah right, only vampires had that power and they're extinct.'

Vampires? What was he talking about? I glanced sideways at Jamie and he gave me a look to suggest that he too had no idea what his dad was talking about.

'Extinct?' Mr Silverman scoffed. 'Are you sure about that?'

A woman entered the lounge through the door from the kitchen. A beautiful woman with long dark hair. She looked like she was in her forties. She wore a black pencil skirt and a dazzling white ruffled shirt. I couldn't help but notice her bright red heels, which were twice the height of anything I would ever attempt to walk in. She looked powerful. Like nothing in the world would scare her.

'I am Veronica,' she said, her voice like silk. 'Leader of the vampires. Or what's left of us anyway.'

Paul's mouth had dropped open. 'But I thought you were all killed?'

'You knew about this?' Jamie asked.

'Not now, Jamie,' his dad replied sharply.

Behind Veronica stood four other people, who I assumed were also vampires. Two men, around the same age as Veronica were stood just behind her. Then behind them there was a younger girl, who looked stunningly beautiful but very serious. Then beside her was …

'Dan?' I couldn't stop myself from saying his name out loud. Luckily no one, except for Jamie, seemed to have heard me. Jamie looked at me with wide eyes.

'Okay, let's get to business,' Mr Silverman said. 'On Monday evening, one of our most loyal men, Garridan, was taken. He was going for a short walk up with street with Candace to build up his strength.' Mr Silverman paused as he shot me an accusing look.

'They bundled him into a white van,' Candace wailed. 'I tried to stop them but we were outnumbered, so I ran. Garridan didn't have the strength.' She looked down at the floor as she caught her breath. She still looked very pale.

My heart missed a beat as realisation dawned. I scanned the room and carefully counted the number of Drifters. They were all there, except one. Garridan must be my dad. My dad had been taken. I tried to signal to Jamie with my eyes but his were fixed firmly on Mr Silverman.

'So,' Jamie said, 'you think that the people who took Ed, also took Garridan? And who exactly are these people? How do we know it wasn't the vampires?' Jamie and Dan scowled at each other.

'Silly boy,' Mr Silverman said, whilst admiring his right hand, which was adorned with silver rings. 'It was the evil humans of course. They have taken them to a secret facility to experiment on them. Treating them like animals. Although, I guess in Ed's case, that's fair enough.'

'Don't you even say Ed's name,' Jamie growled. I wondered whether I would need to hold him back from attacking Mr Silverman, and if I would even have the strength to. Luckily, Jamie managed to control himself.

'How did you find out where they are?' Paul asked.

'Well, that's where Veronica comes in,' Mr Silverman said with a smug smile. 'She reached out to me a few years ago for a favour. A big one. So she owed me. And this seemed like the right time to cash in that favour.'

'So you can help us save them?' I asked. Veronica turned her head slowly and deliberately to look at me.

'Of course,' she said, before licking her lips. 'For a price.'

A chill ran down my spine.

'We have many powers,' Veronica said. 'Invisibility, incredible strength and speed, seer-sight.'

'Seer-sight?' I asked.

'That's how I could see where the humans had taken your friends. It was a haunting image, and I've seen a lot of dark things in my time. They have them strapped to tables … medical instruments everywhere … cages. And the screams.' Veronica shook her head. My stomach lurched.

'But you have no powers without human blood,' Paul said.

Veronica and Mr Silverman looked over at Candace who was slumped against the wall, still breathing heavily.

'Candace was very accommodating,' Veronica said. 'But we need more. And now she is too weak, like the rest of the Drifters.'

'And that's where you come in,' Mr Silverman said waving his hand towards us.

Paul scoffed. 'You've got some nerve. Those vampires aren't coming anywhere near us. Why don't you volunteer yourself?'

'I am a leader. That comes with certain privileges. And I'm the one who has masterminded this whole thing. So now you can play your tiny part and then the vampires will have the strength to rescue Garridan and your little friend, and then everyone can be on their way.'

'No way,' Paul said. 'We'll come up with our own plan. One that doesn't involve blood-sucking.' Paul turned to leave.

'Sure, you go ahead,' Mr Silverman said. 'As long as you have a plan for dodging silver bullets.'

I watched as the colour drained from Paul's face. 'What?'

'Silver bullets. For the benefit of the young ones in the room; they are the only thing that can turn a shapeshifter into a cloud of dust. An untraceable murder. The humans have finally found our weakness. We found some bullets on the floor near where Garridan was taken.' Mr Silverman's expression seemed to soften slightly for the first time, and he looked almost human. 'Listen, I know you have no reason to trust me. But I'm not the bad guy in this situation. I just don't want humans to experiment on and torture our people and get away with it. Think about it, Paul. They will be expecting us to go after them, and they will be ready with their silver bullets. But vampires? They think they killed them all, so they won't be expecting them. The vampires can use their invisibility and strength and don't have to worry about the silver bullets.'

Paul shut his eyes as he considered all that Mr Silverman had said.

'Plus,' Veronica said, 'I am completely willing to kill a human, or two, or three, in order to save your people. Something I'm betting you wouldn't be willing to do yourself.'

'Okay,' Paul said. 'One thing I am sure of, is that Jamie and Mollie are playing no part in this.'

'Dad, we're not kids, let us help,' Jamie said.

'Listen to the boy,' Mr Silverman said with a smirk.

'My decision is final,' Paul growled at Mr Silverman. 'I will sit down and talk with you, and we'll see if we can come to an agreement. But Jamie, and Mollie, you go to another room please. Now.'

'You too,' Veronica said, looking behind her at her vampire tribe. Is tribe the right word? A herd of vampires? A coven maybe?

Jamie put his hand on my back and guided me towards the kitchen. He couldn't bring himself to look at his dad as we passed. Once in the kitchen, Jamie and I stood at one end of the island and the vampires stood at the other. I couldn't help but stare at them. I wanted to see if there was anything unusual about them, but I couldn't find a single thing. No pale skin, no fangs. And I knew from dating Dan that his skin wasn't cold.

Dan was having a hushed conversation with the other vampires, but kept glancing over towards me and Jamie.

Meanwhile, Jamie was fuming. 'I can't believe Dad sent us away. Surely he's not even considering working with vampires. Or trusting a word Mr Silverman says.'

'Jamie … I need to tell you something. I'm pretty sure it's my dad who's been taken.'

'Really? Okay, well I'm sure my dad will figure some-thing out. Try not to worry.'

Dan shuffled down to our end of the kitchen island. He seemed to have lost his usual confident swagger. 'Hey,' he said, seeming almost shy.

Jamie just stared at Dan and puffed out his chest.

'Listen,' Dan said. 'This is all weird for me too. I'm actually a pretty normal guy. Well, apart from the fact I hunt and feed on animals at night. But that's just to keep the cravings at bay, you know. It doesn't give me any powers. Not like human blood would.'

'Did you know about us?' I asked.

'No. I don't have any links to the supernatural world, except occasional contact with Veronica. My dad was a vampire, but my mum's human.'

'Why's your dad not come here today?'

'He's dead. Long story short, vampires worked hard to wean themselves off human blood and hunt only for animals. But when the humans found out about vampires' existence they didn't care about that. They tried to kill us all anyway.'

'I'm so sorry.'

'Thank you.'

This Dan was a much softer version than the one I had got to know at college.

'So, here's a funny story,' I said with a nervous laugh. 'The girl you dated at college called Daisy, that was actually me.'

'Oh really? I liked her, she was cool.'

'You had a funny way of showing it.'

'I don't like to get too close to people. I imagine that if a girl found out I have to hunt for animals every night and drink their blood just to dull the craving for human blood, it would be a bit of a turn-off. And I don't plan on ever starting a family and risk passing on this curse to a child.'

'So the arrogant jock persona is just an act?' I asked.

'Mostly,' Dan said with a grin.

'This is a really lovely catch-up,' Jamie said. 'But all I really want to know is what's being discussed in the other room.'

'Jamie,' I said, 'I already know what your dad's saying. He's not going to want to work with the vampires. I could see the rage Veronica has towards humans. Your dad isn't going to risk unleashing that, even to save Ed and my dad.'

'Your dad's been taken?' Dan asked.

'Yeah,' I said, rubbing my sapphire necklace between my finger and thumb.

'Veronica said the older man in her vision looked in a really bad state.'

A tear ran down my cheek.

'I'm sorry,' Dan said. 'I didn't mean to upset you, I just thought you should know. I would want to know. If it were my dad.'

'Let's not get ourselves worked up,' Jamie said. 'Who says Veronica is telling the truth anyway. My dad will sort it out.'

'Veronica always tells the truth,' Dan said.

'Jamie,' I said. 'Your dad's great. But he's cautious. And I'm worried my dad doesn't have that much time. Can't we come up with our own plan? Like last time?'

'I don't think that's a good idea Mollie,' Jamie replied.

Dan looked at me apologetically. He already knew the pain of losing his father. I wondered if he might be willing to help me. It was worth a try.

'You're right, Jamie. Your dad knows what he's doing. Why don't you go over to the door and try to listen in? I'm just going to get some fresh air.'

As Jamie did as I said, I signalled with my eyes for Dan to follow me outside.

Once outside, Dan took a deep breath. 'Ah. The fresh

air was a good idea.'

'Use my blood,' I blurted out.

'Excuse me?'

'Use it. Use as much as you need to get your powers so you can save my dad and Ed.'

'Mollie, you heard what Jamie said.'

'And you heard what I said. I'm not waiting around for three stubborn adults to decide their next move whilst my dad is dying.'

That seemed to trigger something in Dan. 'Okay, I'll help you. What's the plan?'

Did I have a plan? Sort of. I rode on the back of Dan's motorbike to the outskirts of London, where Veronica had reported Ed and my dad were being held in a disused farm building. We rode as far as we could, then walked the rest of the way and hid in some nearby trees.

'I'm pretty sure that's the place Veronica described from her vision,' Dan said. 'But I think I see some small windows down the side, I'll go and check. You wait here.'

'No way, I need to see too.'

'Suit yourself.'

We strode silently towards the farm building made from corrugated iron. I stood on tiptoes to look in through the grubby window. Inside there were metal tables, most filled with trays of medical instruments. Two large cages with a filthy blanket in each. But they were otherwise empty.

'There,' Dan whispered, whilst pointing through the

window. 'Right at the back.'

There were six men crowded around two tables. They wore dark blue jumpsuits with utility belts. On each belt there hung a deadly silver gun. As the evil men moved around, I caught a glimpse of the two examination tables. Dad lay on one, strapped in place by metal cuffs around his wrists and ankles. There was a drip attached to his left arm. His eyes were closed and his body looked limp. Ed, however, was squirming on his table, fighting against his restraints. I realised why, as I saw one of the men advance towards him holding a needle and syringe.

I dropped down to the floor. I couldn't watch anymore. Dan led us back to the safety of the trees.

'They're experimenting on them,' I wailed. 'Why?'

'Humans have an innate desire to understand everything. And then to control it. You can change all your bodily cells at will. If humans could harness that power, I imagine it could enable some major medical developments.'

'Are you trying to justify what they're doing?'

'No, of course not. I'm just trying to make sense of it. At least they're not just killing you all in cold blood, like they did with us vampires.'

'I'm sorry.'

'No time for that, we need to save your people.'

I caught Dan glance at my neck. I instinctively pulled my hair forwards, as if it would protect me.

'Have you done this before?' I asked.

'No, never.'

'But you know what you're doing?'

'Yeah … of course.'

'You don't sound very certain.'

'It's just … I've heard it can be hard to stop. With animals it doesn't matter … I just drain all their blood. But I'd rather not do that to you.' Dan smiled nervously.

'I trust you,' I said, pulling back my hair and exposing my neck. I was scared. Petrified. But I needed Dan to believe in himself and to focus.

'Are you sure?' Dan asked, not taking his eyes off my neck.

'If you're sure this will give you the powers you need to get in there and rescue my dad and Ed, then yes, I'm sure.'

Dan edged closer to me. I took off my sapphire necklace and squeezed it in the palm of my right hand. Dan put his warm hands around my bare neck. I closed my eyes and braced myself. Then it felt like two knives had been plunged into my neck. The pain was all-consuming and my knees started to buckle. Dan kept his bite on my neck as we sunk to the ground. Then the pain subsided and a warmth spread through my body. I felt like I was floating. Was I about to pass out? I think I had I lost too much blood.

'Stop,' I tried to whisper, but I'm not sure if any sound came out. 'Please, stop.'

Dan managed to tear himself away from my neck. His

eyes were red and wild, and my blood dripped from his fangs. He quickly turned and ran towards the farm building at super-human speed. After a few seconds he disappeared into thin air. There was a boom as his invisible body burst straight through the side wall of corrugated iron. Frenzied shouts were followed by gun shots. Each one made me flinch. One of the captors came flying out through the hole in the wall. He landed on the ground with a thud. His right leg was at a very awkward angle and he wasn't moving. More gun shots. I put my head down on the grass and tried in vain to block them out.

I felt faint and I couldn't force my eyes to stay open any longer. My fist unclenched and my necklace fell from my hand as I succumbed to unconsciousness.

CHAPTER 21

'MOLLIE? MOLLIE? THAT'S it, open your eyes, you're okay. Just take it easy.'

'Dan?' I croaked.

'No, it's Matthew,' he said, stroking my cheek. 'What on earth happened to you?'

I managed to open my eyes and looked around. I was still in the trees near the farm building, but all the Shifters had somehow appeared. Dan was stood a few metres away, his eyes wide and red. And lying next to me were Dad and Ed. I let out a sigh of relief, but I was still too weak to move.

'I'll tell you what happened,' I heard Jamie snarl. 'He bit her.'

'She let me! I was just trying to help,' Dan said.

'Mollie would let you do anything, if it means saving the people she loves. That doesn't mean you can take advantage of her for your own sick fantasies.'

I had never seen Jamie so enraged. And then he shifted into his panther form. He bared his teeth as he prowled towards Dan. He quickly pounced and I watched helplessly as he should have knocked Dan to the floor in one swift movement. But Dan evaporated into a mist and reappeared a few metres away. Jamie wasn't giving up, but this time when he pounced, Dan sprinted away at the speed of light. Panther Jamie and Dan squared up to each other and then started sprinting towards one another. They collided. Somehow, Dan came out on top. He had panther Jamie pinned to the ground. It didn't look like it should be physically possible.

'Stop,' Matthew shouted at Dan. 'You've proved your point, now let him go.'

Dan climbed off of panther Jamie as he shifted back. Jamie gingerly got to his feet and brushed himself off.

'Mollie?' Dad was calling me. I managed to drag myself over to him.

'Dad, are you okay?'

'Never better,' he said with a laugh, then grimaced in pain. 'I think they took liver samples. It hurts.'

Ed was nearby, being supported to stand by Will.

'And are you okay, Ed?' I asked.

'Yeah, I don't feel too bad. Thanks to your dad. He kept telling them to do the tests on him and to leave me alone.'

Dad just waved his hand, as though his extreme selflessness was nothing.

'Let's get you home, Dad. Me and mum can look after you. She'll be so happy to see you, I can't wait to see her face and then we—'

'Mollie. I can't. I would love to come home, more than anything. But I need to go back to the Drifters.'

'No, Dad. You can't.' I couldn't believe this was happening again.

'Mollie, the Drifters are going to be all out for revenge on humans now, even more than before. And it appears they have the vampires onside. My job is more important now than ever.'

'He's right,' Jamie said, finally taking a break from staring aggressively at Dan.

I didn't know what to say. I just ran my fingers through the grass, trying to locate my necklace which I remembered I had dropped. Once I had found it, Dan walked up behind me and helped me to put it back on. I felt a jolt of pain where the chain lay against my bite wounds. 'Thank you,' I whispered. 'For everything.'

'I can take Mollie's father back to the Drifters' house,' Dan said to the group. 'I need to go back and face Veronica and try to explain what happened.'

'Fine,' Jamie said. 'Whatever gets you out of my sight.'

'Jamie,' Ed said. 'Give him a break. He saved me. I'm not sure exactly what's gone on this evening, but he was incredible. He was like an invisible superhero, beating up all the bad guys and sending them flying across the room.'

'Did you kill them?' Matthew asked Dan, although I sensed he didn't really want to know the answer.

'I … I'm not sure,' Dan admitted.

'We need to get out of here,' Jamie said.

I desperately didn't want to say goodbye to Dad again. Especially when he was looking so weak. We embraced lightly as I didn't want to cause him more pain. Then Dad pulled back and put his hands on my shoulders.

'I love you, Mollie. So much. Thank you for saving me.'

All the words I wanted to say got stuck in my throat as Dan supported Dad under the arm and started to lead him away.

If I had more strength, I would have begged him to stay. But I could barely even stand. Matthew held me up.

'How did you even find me?' I asked Jamie.

'As soon as I noticed you and Dan were missing, I knew exactly what you were up to. I overheard Veronica telling my dad about the location and I got the Shifters to meet me here.'

'You shouldn't have done all this alone,' Amber said. She was staring in horror at the marks on my neck. Ava came running over whilst unwrapping a long woollen scarf from around her neck, and then wrapping it round mine. I smiled at her gratefully.

'I'll take you home now,' Jamie said. I wasn't really in the mood to be told what to do. I was still annoyed with him for not helping me with a plan, and how he had acted with Dan.

'No thanks, I'll go with Matthew,' I said. Matthew looked pleasantly surprised, whilst Jamie tried to look like the rejection didn't bother him at all.

'Suit yourself,' Jamie said with a shrug.

Matthew shifted into his wolf form and I climbed on as he set off back to Tanglewood. My adrenaline had faded and my eyes soon started to close. I must have dozed off because it felt like no time at all until Matthew came to a stop in the woods by my house and gently shook me off his back. Once he had shifted back, he pulled me to my feet and put his hands on my shoulders to steady me. Then he slowly unwrapped the scarf from my neck. He gently inspected my bite marks.

'Mollie,' Matthew said sternly. 'What were you thinking?'

'I was thinking that Ed and my dad were being tortured and I wanted to save them.' I crossed my arms in front of my chest.

'But working with a vampire? You could have been killed. Or worse.'

'Dan just wanted to help. His dad was killed by humans. You know what? I'm beginning to wonder who the real enemy is. Maybe Mr Silverman has a point.'

'Of course there are bad humans in the world, and you already knew that. But it doesn't mean they're all bad.'

'I guess so. I just never could have imagined the level of evil I witnessed this evening. And what's to stop them from coming after one of us again?'

Matthew gave me a hug. 'Don't worry about that now. You should go home and get some rest. And take the day off tomorrow too if you need; I'll cover for you.'

'Thanks, Matthew.'

I wrapped the scarf back round my neck to hide the marks from Mum and hoped she wouldn't notice how ill I suspected I looked.

I opened the front door and tip-toed inside.

'Ah, Mollie, there you are, at last.' Apparently, Mum had been waiting up. 'We were worried sick. Where have you been?'

'We?'

Mum blushed. 'Me and Jeremy.'

Of course. I wished we could go back to the time when "we" just meant me and Mum.

'Good evening, Mollie.' Right on cue, Jeremy and his smug little face stepped into the hallway.

'We actually wanted to share some good news with you this evening,' Mum said, moving closer to Jeremy.

Please, *please* don't be pregnant.

'We're engaged!' she squealed, unable to contain her excitement. She held out her left hand to display her tacky-looking ring.

'And I'm moving in,' Jeremy said with a huge smile.

I didn't know if I was going to faint or vomit. I felt like I had been kicked in the stomach. Twice. Despite my exhaustion, my adrenaline started to kick in again. It was fight or flight. I decided this wasn't a fight I was going win.

'That's so great,' I said with the biggest and most genuine smile I could muster. 'Why don't we all have a drink to celebrate, I'll join you in a second.'

Mum and Jeremy walked hand in hand into the kitchen. Mum was acting so differently, I barely recognised her. How could she do this to Dad? Jeremy was the complete opposite of him.

I turned and opened the front door silently. And then I ran. The cold air hitting my face felt so good. But then my breathing became steadily faster and heavier until I was forced to stop and rest. Stupid blood loss. I flagged down a taxi and said the first address that came to my mind.

I stared out of the window of the taxi as the bright streetlights whizzed past in a blur. I thought about Dad and the torture that the humans had put him through. I thought about Mum and how Jeremy had changed her. I thought about Dan losing his dad because humans were afraid of what they didn't understand and couldn't control.

I walked up to the front door and knocked loudly three times.

I didn't have to wait long.

'Mollie. What a pleasant surprise.' But Mr Silverman held two glasses of champagne in his hands, suggesting he already knew I was coming.

'Veronica saw that I would be coming here? I didn't even know myself until minutes ago.'

'It's not important how I knew you'd be here, but rather that you are here. What can I do for you, Mollie?'

'You said you had a plan? To take control of the country from the humans.'

'That I did.'

'Well, I'm in. I want to help. Just tell me what I need to do.'

Mr Silverman grinned from ear to ear. 'Come on in, Mollie. Make yourself at home.' He handed me a glass of champagne. 'It's time to fulfil your destiny.'

Author's Note

I cannot thank you enough for taking the time to read my debut novel. If you have enjoyed immersing yourself in Mollie's world as much as I have, then I will be over the moon. I would be so grateful if you would consider writing a review or recommending to a friend.

Printed in Great Britain
by Amazon